PUF

The Sighting

Jan Mark grew up in Kent and attended the Canterbury College of Art. She went on to teach art at Gravesend. She started her writing career in 1974, and since then has written a large number of highly successful books, which have won numerous prestigious prizes including the Carnegie Medal. She spent two years as writer-in-residence at Oxford Polytechnic and now lives in Oxford.

Chapter One

Mum said, 'You don't have to come with us if you don't want to.' It was the third time she had said it and they would be leaving in less than an hour.

'I do want to,' Jack said. 'I keep telling you I do. I've never been to one before.'

'Well, it's not going to be a laugh a minute,' Mum said. 'I should think you'd be bored out of your skull, and anyway it's freezing. Why don't you stay here and watch videos, get a take-away –'

'I didn't get off the last day at school to watch videos,' Jack said. 'I want to come with you; it's you that don't want me to. Marty's going. Why do I always get left out?'

'We're going to a funeral, not Alton Towers,' Dad said. 'What do you think you'll be missing?'

'He's seen too many funerals on telly,' Marty said. 'He thinks it'll be like in movies, with people getting drunk and fighting and falling into the grave.'

'That's Shakespeare, not movies. You're thinking of *Hamlet.*'

'Given *your* family,' Mum said, 'that's very likely what will happen. If I'd known that I was marrying into a blood feud I would have turned you down flat and run off with Chris Monroe.'

It was an old joke that Mum had married Peter Aylward only because she could not face becoming Marilyn Monroe, but it was the first that Jack had heard of any blood feud, although odd facts had been coming to light during the last few days since the telephone call. An unfamiliar man's voice had announced to Dad that he thought they might be cousins, and then, when they had worked out that this was the case, had told him that their grandfather was dead – Dad's grandfather, Jack's great-grandfather; his only great-grandfather. He had a stake in this.

'Look, it's *my* great-grandad,' he said. 'I want to go to his funeral.'

'But you never met him. *I* never met him.'

'That's why I want to go. We could see him in his coffin.'

'Ghoul,' Marty said. 'That's the real reason. He wants to see a dead person.'

'If that's how things are, perhaps you'd better stay at home.'

'Movies again,' Marty chanted. 'It's not going to be one of those American coffins with a hinge and everybody filing past to say goodbye to the dear departed lying there, all done up in frills like a birthday cake.'

'Perhaps you'd better *both* stay here . . .'

'We're all going,' Dad said. 'Aren't we, Lyn?' He put his arm round Mum. 'Family solidarity?'

'Chance would be a fine thing,' Mum said. 'Family solidarity? Fifty people not speaking to each other; I can't wait.'

'What's a blood feud, then?' Jack asked Marty later, in the back of the car. Marty was reading. Jack had been looking out of the window at the blue ice-filled woods beside the motorway, but now the traffic was decelerating, crawling uphill into freezing fog, and there was nothing to see but hazard warning signs flashing at intervals. Even the London-bound head-lights were invisible, a few metres to the right across the central reservation and detected only by a shifting glow. Jack had brought a book of his own to read, although he always felt sick in cars if he lowered his eyes. In front of him Mum was hugging her shoulders, her fingertips digging into the cable stitches on her sweater, a sure sign that she was nervous. Nervous about the fog or about the funeral? He thought that he had better not ask.

'You say something?' Marty looked up from her page. She would never allow herself to be interrupted while she was reading, but if someone spoke to her she would put the remark on hold, finish the paragraph or page, or even the chapter, retrieve and answer, sometimes minutes later. It was no good repeating yourself or shouting. Jack had a mental picture of Marty behind a counter, protected by soundproof glass, where people queued up obediently until she was ready for them.

'A blood feud. What's a blood feud?'

3

'Oh, a quarrel that goes on for years, between families usually. Someone insults somebody else, and then the person who was insulted kills the first one to get back at him, and then the dead man's family kill the murderer to even things up and then the murderer's family avenge him by killing one of the other lot – it goes on for centuries sometimes, like, you know, *Romeo and Juliet*.'

'No, I don't know Romeo and Juliet. Friends of yours?'

'The Montagues and the Capulets – killing each other to avenge the family honour. Well, that's the excuse. In the play it's just two bunches of yobbos looking for a fight.'

'I thought you said *Hamlet*. Anyway, that's two families, Montagues and Capulets. And our lot aren't killing each other, are they? Nobody murdered Great-Grandad.'

'Keep your voice down,' Marty said, twitching an eyebrow at Mum's burrowing fingers. 'You know what it's like with big families, one half never speaking to the other half.'

'And not killing each other either,' Jack muttered, as Marty bent her head and began reading again. He suspected that Marty's knowledge of big families came out of books. He had always been vaguely aware that somewhere over the horizon were relatives that they had never met; but wasn't that true of most people? It was only in soaps, on the box, that people kept turning up to reveal themselves as long-lost uncles, cousins, fathers, younger brothers and sisters, even, who had never been mentioned before. In any case, that usually

4

seemed to happen in Australia. Things were different out there. They had more room to get lost in.

This was the real reason that he wanted to go to the funeral, to catch a sight of these unknown and unfriendly relatives.

They would not be fighting around the graveside, of course they would not. They would be icily polite, grinning frigidly and kissing the air over each other's shoulders.

Anyway, he had never been to a funeral, you had to start somewhere. Granny and Grandpa, Mum's parents, were still alive, quite young. Grandpa rode a motorbike, Granny played tennis, they were both swimmers, healthy, would be around for years. He did not want to think of them dying. Better to start with someone you did not know, someone very old and very distant. And yet that someone was Dad's own grandpa, who must once have been young enough to swim, to play tennis, who had married and had the son who grew up to become Dad's father; who had once been younger than that, a child himself, someone else's grandson.

Someone who had been part of a little family like his own –

'Marty?' He could see by her book that the chapter was ending, so she would be answering in a minute or two. While he waited, he reared up and stared over Mum's shoulder at the grey wet windscreen, the fog beyond it so opaque that it seemed to be part of the glass. The car had been grinding along at not much more than a walking pace for so long that he was surprised to notice that now they were going downhill, and at the same moment the windscreen began to lighten. The fog became a golden haze.

'Watch it. This is where it gets really dangerous,' Mum was saying. 'Everyone starts accelerating.'

And then the fog was gone. They were plunging through a sheer curved cutting between vertical chalk cliffs, and below them lay a sunlit plain, white with thin frozen snow as far as they could see, a view that ended in blue haze and a plume of white cloud above a faraway cluster of chimneys and cooling towers.

'It was almost worth coming for this,' Mum said, fumbling in the glove locker for the sunglasses she had not worn since September.

'Where are we?' Jack said. He had never imagined that anywhere in England could look like this.

'The Oxford Plain, Thames Valley; that must be Didcot Power Station,' Dad said. 'We're forty minutes behind schedule but we ought just to make it.'

'Especially if we don't miss the turning,' Mum said, 'which is just coming up – Junction 6, for Watlington.'

Marty finally looked up. 'What?'

'Watlington.'

'Not you, Mum,' Marty said pleasantly. 'Jack said something earlier.'

'What d'you call a family with just a mum and a dad and the children?'

'Nuclear,' Marty said and turned to the next chapter.

'Why?' Jack said quickly, before she could start reading again. 'Why nuclear?'

'Nucleus – basic unit. Just enough to call it a family. We're nuclear.'

'I know.'

6

'If you count all the grannies and uncles and cousins and that, it's an extended family.'

'Thermonuclear,' Mum said bitterly. 'With a half-life of a century and fall-out even unto the tenth generation.'

'Well, the snow's much worse north of Leicester,' Dad said. 'Half of them may be stuck on the M1.'

'Yes, but which half, the Ackroyds or the Cowgills?'

'Were the Ackroyds involved?'

'They must have sided with someone or we'd *know* if they were involved. We'd know *them*.'

'Maybe they'll decide to call it a day and we'll go home bosom chums,' Dad said. 'Time the great healer and all that.'

'If you ask me, time's had the reverse effect on this mob.' Mum had the road map out again. 'And you'll need to take the next left turn.'

Marty said suddenly, 'Do you think it would have made any difference if *your* dad hadn't lost touch?'

Mum said 'No' grimly. Dad said 'Probably', but neither of them went on and the conversation dozed off. Marty was reading again. Jack looked at them all, filled with suspicion. Marty knew something that he did not. Marty knew a lot of things that he did not, which was fair enough, she was older. But this was something that Mum or Dad must have told her, told *her* and not told him.

'I'm sure I see an olive branch waving in the wind,' Dad said. 'Otherwise, why would they have bothered to let us know? They could have had the funeral without our ever finding out.'

'It might have been in the papers.'

'Why on earth would it be in the papers?'

'Celebrated scandal, family riven by age-old controversy.'

'I doubt if anyone's interested enough. If it was that celebrated, we'd know about it.'

'They were interested once,' Mum said. 'Hence the scandal.'

'All that effort gone into hushing it up. They'd hardly let it out now.'

'Whatever it was,' Mum said, just as Jack was saying, 'What was it?'

'One of my uncles,' Dad said, 'saw things.'

'What sort of things?'

'Aliens at the bottom of the garden,' Mum said.

'Did he really?' Jack said. 'Really see aliens? What were they like?'

'Nobody knows,' Mum said, 'but there was one hell of a row and a family bust-up.'

'Because he saw aliens?'

'I wish you hadn't said anything,' Mum complained to Dad. 'Next turn right, then first left, and slow down. It's getting foggy again. Jack, for God's sake don't say anything about aliens to anyone. I mean, you probably won't get the chance to say anything anyway, but aliens are definitely off-limits.'

'I don't think they called them aliens in those days,' Dad said. 'They were known as little green men.'

'The modern ones are grey,' Marty said. 'They are very slow learners. They keep on abducting humans and conducting experiments, but they still don't seem to know how we work. Isn't that the church?'

Over the shoulder of a hill a weathercock rose up

as though it were stuck into the hillside itself. They had turned at the entrance of a narrow lane with cars parked all along one side, leaving almost no room to pass. Dad pulled in behind the last car. The lane ran downhill and turned slightly at the foot. The hedges stood high on either side and the top of the church tower, from which the weathercock really was growing, was only just visible through a gap. The clock face on it read 11.25.

'We've got five minutes,' Dad said. 'Get a move on.'

Marty was climbing out of the back, very slowly, finishing her paragraph.

'It's only quarter-past,' she said, without looking up. 'It's probably been 11.25 here for years.'

'We can sneak in at the back,' Mum said, 'and sneak out again if things look bad. We can't hurry anyway, the road's like glass.'

'Let's hold on to each other.'

'Like mountaineers roped together who all fall down the same crevasse? Get the wellies out of the boot and we can change back again in the porch. I'm not ice-skating in heels.'

'We ought to go to more funerals,' Marty said, putting the book in her coat pocket. 'Then we'd know how to behave. I went to church with Cassy Philips last week so I'd get some idea of what goes on, but it wasn't a funeral. They were all clapping and singing and shaking hands. Mind you, they might do that at funerals too.'

'I don't need wellies,' Jack said. He was wearing his school shoes with soles like tyre treads. He left the others hopping about on one foot and set off down the lane, getting a good look at the cars as he went. They were an impressive collection: BMWs, Peugeots, Volvos, Range Rovers, mostly, with this year's plates. Their own old Renault was in the right place, up at the back where no one would notice it. They would not have any difficulty reversing out again either, being so near to the junction. He wondered if the others were going to back out as well. The four-wheel drives would be all right, but the rest were going to be in trouble, reversing uphill on this frozen slope.

He reached the bend and the first of the ordinary cars at the same moment. Around the corner were the undertaker's black limousines and the hearse, drawn up alongside the stone wall of the churchyard. Meandering organ music thrummed inside the church. In the porch was a clergyman in a white surplice, glancing at his wristwatch, and a small, elderly, angry-looking woman, all in black, who darted out waving her arms when Jack went through the gate.

'You can't come in here, there's a service going on.'

'We've come for the funeral,' Jack said, realizing as he spoke that he had made it sound as if they were arriving at a party. 'The others are just behind,' he added, as Mum, Dad and Marty skidded round the bend. They were laughing. The woman looked angrier than ever and crunched down the gravel path to the gate.

'Who are you? Who is it?'

Dad stepped forward. 'Peter Aylward,' he said.

The little woman stared at him, not smiling. 'An Aylward?'

It was evidently the wrong thing to be.

Dad pressed on bravely. 'This is my wife, Lyn, and these are Martina and Jack. And you are . . . ?'

The woman still did not smile. At last she said, 'Patricia Cowgill.'

'Patricia?' Dad seemed to be dredging up a long-forgotten memory. 'Are you Auntie Pat?'

The woman had been snapping-angry, now she was furious. 'What are you doing here?'

'Same as you, Auntie Pat,' Dad said cheerfully. 'Come to bury Grandad. Don't let's hang about out here, it's too cold.'

Mum was smiling nicely and holding out her hand to Auntie Pat. Whose auntie? Dad's? Why had they never heard of her before? In any case, Auntie Pat was not going to shake Mum's hand. She was looking at it as if Mum were offering her a dead fish. Marty stumped past them all and into the church porch, where she sat down, tugged off her boots and put her shoes on. Jack followed her, looking over his shoulder to see how Mum and Dad were handling Auntie Pat, but they had given up and were hurrying behind him.

'Silly old bat,' Mum was saying. Jack reflected that if it was loud enough for him to hear, no doubt Auntie Pat had heard it too. He knew that he would always think of her now as Auntie Bat and hoped that he would never meet her again in case he had to speak to her and it slipped out by accident.

Mum sat down on the porch bench beside Marty and changed into her shoes.

'Well, that was a good start,' she muttered. 'I said so, didn't I? Didn't I say it? Fifty people not speaking to each other – and she's the first.'

The vicar had gone inside the church, but now he put his head round the door. 'I think you'll find room near the back,' he said. He looked nervous and shot out of sight again as Auntie Pat stamped across the echoing stone floor, sounding like a staple gun, and pushed past him into the church.

'Oh, well,' Dad said, smiling dismally, 'last in, first out. We can make a quick getaway afterwards.' He pushed at the heavy wooden door that Auntie Pat had left swinging and they tiptoed behind him.

It was dimly pale and chilly in the nave, like being inside a cheese dish. Jack found himself looking straight down the aisle to the chancel steps, where a coffin, with one wreath on it, was resting on a trestle table. The aisle was short and the pews each side looked crowded with people who seemed to have divided themselves into two opposing teams. On the right everyone was wearing ordinary clothes, winter coats and sweaters. On the left they were all in black and the women had hats. Jack was sure that his family belonged to the lighter side with the bare heads and sweaters, but the pews were filled. The only space seemed to be in the second row from the back among the black coats and hats. Auntie Pat was stapling up and down the aisle, peering into pews to see if she could find somewhere suitable to stow them and she did, up at the front, near the coffin. She was bobbing and waving and pointing, but Mum took no notice and slipped into the second-to-last pew next to a woman in a black fur coat with more fur round her hat. Dad followed uncertainly, but Marty was pushing him into position and he could not escape.

There was no room for Jack, who had hovered too long.

'Go up the front,' Marty hissed.

Jack looked at Auntie Pat, who was angrily beckoning him to do just that, and shook his head.

'Chair,' he mouthed at Marty and went to sit in a place he had noticed as he came in, a chair on the other side of the door, with a radiator beside it and a red curtain behind.

He sat down just as the vicar reappeared on the chancel steps and began to speak, welcoming all those who had come from near and far to say farewell to Robert John Aylward.

He jumped. It was his own name, scrambled. He was John Robert Aylward. For the first time he felt some real connection with whoever it was who lay in the coffin up there in front of the altar.

'All of us who knew Robert . . .' the vicar was saying. Jack switched off again. He did not know Robert. He had never known Robert. Now he never would know Robert. In a little while Robert was going into that hole out there by the yew tree. He had seen the mound of earth as he approached the church, but had not taken it in that this marked the grave.

He shivered. How miserable to be buried on such a bleak and stony day as this, hurried on his way by people like crabby Auntie Pat, the fidgety vicar and some other unseen person who was distantly coughing, on and on, an especially funereal cough.

He leaned against the radiator only to discover that it was not hot. It was not even warm, but icy cold and sweating slightly. Then he realized that the red cylinders in the aisle, with what looked like rakes inverted above them, were propane gas bottles with heaters attached. All the warmth was directed away from him.

There was a vicious draught leaking under the door. He wondered if anyone would notice if he were to drape the red curtain over his shoulders or wrap it round his legs like a travelling rug, and tweaked it to see what lay on the far side.

He had thought it would be another door, but instead he was looking into a square empty room lit by a high pointed window. It was the bottom of the tower.

He thought of slipping behind the curtain and doing some silent exercises to warm up. The organ was playing again. Everyone was standing. No one would hear him, they were going to sing a hymn.

Jack stood up too, unnoticed. Mum, Dad and Marty were singing, or going through the motions. He could tell by the way their heads were moving. And, although the vicar was facing his way, he was hidden from sight by the people standing between them. He could vanish, magically, and nobody would know where he had gone.

Something touched him between the shoulders and he started. He must have leaned on a bit of projecting stone, or a shelf, or – but the curtain was behind him and there was nothing behind the curtain.

Jack felt his skin creep. He had heard of people's hair standing on end with fright – you saw it in cartoons, great shocks of terrified fuzz – but now he knew it was not the hair on your head that stood on end; it was the hair on your arms and legs and neck, rising up like the fur on a frightened cat.

And then a pale, thin hand came round the curtain and rested on his shoulder and a hoarse voice said, 'Well, are you coming in or not?' The voice smelled of throat pastilles and the hand had a felt-tip doodle on the thumbnail. Without another thought, Jack left his place and backed behind the curtain.

Chapter Two

The owner of the hand seemed to belong to the team in the black strip. He wore black trousers, black jacket, black shirt and a white tie. With his dark hair combed back and his pale face half hidden by mirror shades, he looked like a kind of hippie gangster.

As the organ music and the singing drowned every other sound, he did not lower his voice when he said, 'I'm Julius Aylward, great-grandson of the deceased.' He coughed discreetly. 'Who you?'

'I'm his great-grandson too. Did you say Jools?'

'*Not* Jools. Julius.'

'I'm Jack Aylward.'

'Short for John? Were you named after GG?'

'Who?'

'Great-Grandfather.'

'I might have been, but I didn't even know his name till just now. He was Robert John, I'm John Robert and so was my grandfather, Dad says.'

'Keep your voice down. The hymn's ending.'

'How do you know?'

'It's only got three verses.'

'How d'you know that?'

'Because I know it. Do you want to go out again and pray, or come and get warm?'

'I'll come and get warm. Where?'

Julius jerked his head. 'Upstairs.'

Across one corner of the tower's square space was a door, pointed like the window and designed for midgets. 'Quick,' Julius hissed, as the sound of the organ died away, 'while they're all sitting down again.'

Under cover of the roaring shuffle that drifted through the curtain, he turned the door handle and pushed Jack through into the little dark space beyond. It was the foot of a spiral staircase that coiled upward, lit only by miserly slit windows. Julius closed the door silently, removed his shades and said, 'Go on up.'

The stair was so steep and shadowy that Jack put his hands down and went up on all fours, like a dog. The stones beneath his fingers were colder than the radiator had been and he wondered what he was doing, what he had let himself in for, climbing a church tower in the dead of winter with the strange black-clad youth who shared his name. That had not struck him at the time – they were both Aylwards.

There was no door at the head of the stairs. Suddenly it grew lighter and he rose out of the cold gloom into another square room with a high ceiling. From a square hole in the middle of it hung four fat ropes with furry ends that were looped up against the wall. It was warm. Under the window was an ornate electric fire, apparently dating from the fifteenth century, with one glowing bar. Not very much light came in at the window and when Jack peered through it, expecting to see hills and woods, he discovered that he had lost all sense of direction crawling up the spiral staircase. The window looked down into the nave, at the two teams of mourners, the All Blacks and The Rest, the vicar and the coffin.

'This is where the bell-ringers would be, if there were any bell-ringers,' Julius said, coming up behind him.

'How do you know about it?'

'I often come up here. I live here.'

'In the church?'

'In Stoke Crowell. We lived with Great-Grandad; someone had to look after him.'

Jack stared down through the small panes of thick green glass. 'Which side are you on? The All Blacks or The Rest?'

'Side?' Julius followed his gaze. 'I'm with Jilly and Steve. They're up at the front, chief mourners, sort of. On the end of the front pew on the left. My parents. Jilly's in the red coat.'

'They look like they ought to be with The Rest.'

'All Blacks are family,' Julius said.

'You're dressed to match.'

'I just like wearing black. This is a good excuse to go all out.'

'Why aren't you down there, then, where everyone can see you?'

'I've got a bad cough at the moment but I didn't want to miss it, so I came up here. Have a Fisherman's

Friend. It's funny how they've split into two like that. Where are the rest of your lot?'

'In the second pew up. We look like we ought to be with The Rest, but we came in late.'

'I know,' Julius said. 'I watched you. When I saw you disappear I thought you might be going to sneak out the back so I came down to meet you. If you're an Aylward you ought to be with the All Blacks. What's your father's name?'

'Peter.'

'And his father was John, you say?' Julius took out a pencil and was starting to draw some kind of a diagram on the whitewashed wall. 'Your father and my father are cousins,' he said. 'That makes us second cousins, or cousins twice removed, or something. But kin, definitely kin.'

Down below the organ boomed into life again and the congregation stood up. '"Eternal Father Strong to Save",' Julius said. 'That's because of the Navy.'

'What Navy?'

'The Royal Navy. GG was a captain of corvettes during World War Two, escorting Atlantic convoys. "Eternal Father strong to save, whose arm doth guide the restless wave." Didn't you know that?'

'I don't know anything. I don't know anyone,' Jack said. 'I've never seen any of them before.'

'Nor've I. Well, not most of them, anyway. "Let's see who comes out of the woodwork now," Jilly said, when they put the notice in the paper.'

'I didn't think there was a notice in the paper,' Jack said, recalling the conversation in the car.

'The *Telegraph*, because she thought that was the one

that all the uncles and aunties and other dinosaurs would read. How did you find out, then?'

'Someone phoned Dad.'

'Steve probably. He was the one who wanted to get everybody together. I don't think it'll work, though,' Julius added.

'The blood feud?'

'That's our name for it.' Julius sounded put out. 'Who told you?'

'No one. It's just something Mum said. She didn't want to come because she said it would be fifty people not speaking to each other.'

'She was close. Forty-three, I counted them in; eighteen All Blacks – The Rest are locals. And she was right, they aren't speaking to each other except to be rude. Auntie Pat has insulted everyone on both sides.'

'Is she your auntie?'

'Not properly. I think she's GG's niece. And people get called auntie and uncle even when they aren't related to you at all.'

'*Why* aren't they speaking to each other? What happened?'

'We don't know,' Julius said. 'But it must have been something long ago and very horrible.'

'But your dad's all right, isn't he? Mine is. Why don't *they* speak to each other?'

'Oh, that's easy,' Julius said. 'We didn't even know you existed except that someone thought there were relatives down in Kent. Steve made some rapid inquiries. That's what Jilly meant about people coming out of the woodwork, all these people we'd never heard of. I don't mean that you, and them –' he pointed at Mum, Dad and Marty – 'that you came out of the woodwork, but you know, till this last week it was just me and Jilly and Steve and Great-Grandad and now, suddenly, look, it's all that lot, the All Blacks, and they're *all* our relatives and they all hate each other and no one knows why.'

'What about Auntie Pat?'

'We think she knows,' Julius said, 'and if everyone didn't hate *her* before they will after this.'

'But they don't *really* hate each other, do they?' Jack said. 'I mean, mostly they're like us, aren't they – didn't even know about each other?'

The hymn had ended and people were sitting down again. A bearded man left his place at the front, next to the woman in the red coat. It was Julius's father, Steve, who went out on to the chancel steps to speak. Jack strained to hear what he said but the thick glass in the little window muffled his voice.

'We'll soon find out,' Julius said. 'You're coming back afterwards, aren't you?'

'Back where?'

'To the manor, for lunch. Everyone's invited.'

'You live in a manor house?'

'It was Great-Grandad's house,' Julius said. 'And he didn't leave it to us. We've got to clear out. Look, things are moving.'

What was moving was the coffin. Six men in dark coats had lifted it on to their shoulders and were walking slowly down the aisle. From either side people edged out of their pews and followed it, led by Julius's Jilly and Steve. From among the All Blacks, Auntie Pat shot out of her place at the front and elbowed her way ahead of them.

'You see how it is,' Julius said. 'Pat never came near the place when he was alive, but she's jealous. I suppose she'd known him the longest. Poor Great-Grandad.'

'Will you miss him?' Jack said.

'I didn't see much of him,' Julius said. 'He didn't really know who we were – he was ninety-five, remember. He had a nurse at the end – that's her behind Steve. We just looked after the house. I'll miss the house. We'd better go down now.' He switched off the electric fire. 'It's for the bell-ringers – was. No one rings the bells these days. It's probably a fire hazard; the plug's hot. So, are you coming back for lunch?'

'I think we're going home,' Jack said. 'I don't know. I'd better find the others. Where's the house?'

'Through the churchyard. It's got its own way in. Don't leave yet. I'm going to the grave for the interment. Just follow everyone else. See you later.'

They trod carefully down the spiral staircase, in which Julius's cough echoed hollowly. Jack noticed that he had a key to lock the door behind them. On the far side of the curtain the nave was murmurous with footsteps and quiet voices. Julius slipped round it and by the time Jack followed him he had vanished among the shuffling adults. He waited until the church was almost empty before sidling out to join Mum and Dad and Marty.

'Where did you get to?' Marty demanded. 'I looked round and you'd vanished.'

'You weren't fooling around, were you?' Mum said anxiously. 'I guessed you'd nipped behind the curtain.'

'Just getting out of the draught – there's no heating at the back,' Jack said, thinking that perhaps going up the tower would count as fooling about. 'I met somebody.'

'Ay, ay, what's all this, then?' Marty leered. 'Secret trysts behind the arras. What are we going to do, Dad? Whip out fast like you said or go over to the house for funeral baked meats?'

'Let's get out now, while we can,' Mum said. 'I don't think I want another round with Auntie Pat.'

'We can easily lose her among this crowd,' Dad said. 'Anyway, she'll have gone to the graveside. Didn't you see her barging ahead to be first in the queue?'

'You *want* to stay.'

'Well, I wouldn't mind a look at the house, while we're here. Or a look at the family. Just for half an hour?'

'I'll wait in the car,' Mum said. 'You don't want to go over there, do you, Marty?'

'I do,' Jack said. 'Anyway, I thought that's why we came, to meet them.'

They were on the gravel patch by the porch. The sunlight had been entirely blotted out by fog that had rolled down from the hills during the service. People stood around in shivering groups with steam rising above their heads, like Didcot Power Station.

'Look at them all,' Marty said. 'They'd rather stand out here and freeze than be the first to move.'

'I know how they feel,' Mum said, but at last two of The Rest made a move and gradually people began walking along a grass path between the graves, to a small gate in the far side of the churchyard wall.

'Come on,' Dad said. 'A bite to eat and a hot drink and then we'll go home. The fog may have shifted in an hour.'

'It was half an hour just now,' Mum said, but all the same they began to follow the other people towards the gate. Jack looked round. Where before he had seen a mound of earth, there was now a small huddle of mourners, one slightly shorter than the others: Julius. The vicar, with a cloak over his white surplice, stood at one end, speaking, and the fog drifted drearily round them. Someone was coughing, long and hard. Julius again, Jack guessed.

On the other side of the gate a narrow path led uphill between frosted yew bushes clipped close into two dark, solid walls. Then they came out at the far end into a garden that was so sheltered, snow still lay on the trees and hedges. Ahead of them was the house. Jack had somehow expected a mansion, but it was just a house, big, not enormous; long, with a steep roof and many windows. They were approaching it from the back and the procession, of which they were the tail, was snaking round to the front, where big double gates led out on to the road. At the head of shallow stone steps was a porch with open doors.

'He must have been worth a bit, our great-grandad,' Marty said, not very quietly, 'if this was his house. I wonder who'll inherit it?'

'It'll probably go to close family. There were a couple of cousins who looked after him. And do keep your voice down, Marty,' Dad said. 'There's sure to be a row before long and it would be a pity if we caused it.'

Jack wanted to say, 'Those cousins, they won't get

the house,' but did not. He was realizing that after his short talk with Julius he actually knew more about the family set-up than his parents did.

A woman whom he had seen in the church was standing by the front door, smiling professionally. 'Coats to the left, there's a sign on the door. Bathrooms are clearly marked. Please go through to the right when you are ready.' She sounded like someone in a theatre, checking tickets and directing people to their seats. Perhaps she was selling programmes.

'Bath*rooms*,' Marty said. 'Have we hit pay dirt?'

Dad collected their coats and took them away. Mum went upstairs to look for the loo. 'And to case the joint,' Marty said, before sprinting after her. Jack walked down a corridor and into a long room filled with people. Tables of food stood to one side, under windows that overlooked the garden. Opposite was a wide open fireplace with logs burning in it. A voice in the crowd was saying, 'Please do help yourself to eats. Drinks are on that table at the end.'

Another voice was saying, 'Nellie was my aunt, of course,' and someone else, close to Jack, said meanly, 'If I were Nellie's niece I'd stay quiet about it.'

A third voice laughed unkindly.

'Keep a low profile,' Dad said. 'Grab a plateful and sit down out of the way. Get yourself a drink.'

Jack loaded a plate with sandwiches and bits of cooked birds and crumby things on skewers. He treated himself to a glass of white wine because he occasionally had it at home and knew that it would not be too disgusting. People were standing around in clusters, as they had done outside the church, eyeing each other up and muttering among themselves. Jack squeezed between them and returned to the fireplace. Round the hearth, which was at least two metres wide, stood a brass fender like a fence, with red leather seats at either end and at the corners. Jack took one right against the wall and sat with his feet in the hearth. He was safely out of the way of elbows and from here he could keep an eye on the door, watching for Julius.

He felt even more warm and comfortable thinking of the little group in the churchyard, standing round the open grave. Almost he felt sorry for them, but they would be inside soon enough. It was his great-grandfather, Robert John Aylward, who would be staying outside, who would never come into the warm again.

He saw Mum and Marty heading for the food. Dad was going round the room with a fixed smile, introducing himself to people. No one looked very pleased to see him. Jack noticed that gradually the groups of people were doing what they had done in church, taking sides, the All Blacks and The Rest. Now he began to see why. The All Blacks were older. They had grown up at a time when everyone wore black for funerals. They were smarter, wealthier, older and angrier. The Rest were not young – he and Marty were the only really young ones in the room – but they were younger than the All Blacks. The All Blacks had sided against The Rest, and The Rest were huddling together for protection.

The Rest all looked different from each other, not only because they were wearing ordinary clothes. Their hair and features were different. But the All Blacks were white- or grey-headed. Just being old made them look alike. Marty stood out among them with her gingery curls and the harlequin jacket that she had sewn herself out of velvet patchwork. Jack wondered who he looked like, because he was at least related to some of these people, to Julius for a start. Marty wasn't related to anyone, but the people who were gazing at her curiously could not know that she was adopted.

In the hall, voices were raised and a cough rang out as the people who had been at the graveside came in with the vicar. There was a row going on, Jack could see, with Auntie Pat at the centre of it. Julius's mum, Jilly, looked as if she had been crying and his father had his mouth set in a long thin line of rage between moustache and beard.

The groups began to reassemble and tighten up, voices turned down to an ill-natured grumble. Jack heard Mum, somewhere close, saying, 'The sooner we leave, the better. It's like waiting for an earthquake when all the birds stop singing.' Dad caught his eye and nodded towards the door. Mum was tapping Marty on the shoulder. Within seconds they were all standing in the hall.

'Get the coats,' Mum said to Dad, 'and then let us get the hell out. I have never seen such a gruesome collection in all my life . . .'

Jack looked round for Julius. He had not gone into the long room with the others, but on a table near the front door Jack saw a pair of mirror shades and a white woollen tie wrapped around them.

Dad came back with the coats. 'Shall we say goodbye?'

'Who to?' Mum said. 'They'll all be at each other's throats before long. We won't be missed. Don't forget we have to pick up our boots from the porch as we go through the churchyard.'

'What's this place called?' Jack asked, as they hurried through the garden and down the alley between the yews.

'Stoke Crowell Manor,' Dad said, 'I suppose.'

'What county's it in?'

'Bucks or Oxfordshire, I'm not sure. The county boundary's along here somewhere.'

Jack wondered if a letter to 'Julius Aylward, Stoke Crowell Manor, Bucks or Oxfordshire' would ever arrive. It seemed wrong to rush away without saying anything to him; he might be hurt. Julius had not looked particularly fragile but Jack would have been hurt in his place. 'See you later,' he had said. Why had he not come in with the others? Had Auntie Pat been hateful to him too? Between them they could have dealt with Auntie Pat.

He and Dad waited while Mum and Marty changed back into their boots. The air was very slightly warmer; the fog was turning to rain, but freezing as it fell, as they straggled up the hill past the row of cars. There were already gaps. They were not even the first to leave.

In the car Mum took out the road atlas and found their location. 'We needn't even reverse,' she said. 'This lane goes on round the church and rejoins the B481. It must be the same one that passes the manor. Perhaps we can wing somebody on the way past.'

'I'm sorry,' Dad said. 'Sorry to drag you all this way.

It was worse than I thought it could possibly be. I had hoped . . .' He turned the key in the ignition. Nothing happened.

'I don't believe this,' Mum said. 'Out of fuel? Dead battery? Did you leave the lights on?'

He tried again. 'Starter motor's jammed.'

'Is that something we can fix?' Jack said.

'No, it isn't.' He sat and swore softly. 'I'd try a coasting start, but not on this surface and not with that Cavalier ten feet away.'

'Hit it,' Marty advised.

'Did anyone see a garage on the way?' Mum asked.

'Not in walking distance,' Dad said. 'We'll have to phone the AA.'

'Said you ought to get a mobile,' Marty sighed. 'Did anyone see a phone box?'

'Won't someone give us a tow?' Jack said.

'This lot?' Down the lane rear lights were glowing and cars were leaving. 'Anyway, in these weather conditions I don't want to risk emergency surgery.'

'I'll go and ring from the house,' Jack said, thinking of a chance to see Julius again. 'Or get them to ring.'

'Is that wise?' Mum said.

'Wiser than sitting here freezing,' Dad said. 'Come on, Jack, let's give it a whirl.'

Chapter Three

As the churchyard came into view, they saw a pack of assorted All Blacks and The Rest straggling between the graves, from the gate in the far wall.

'We'll go the other way,' Dad said; 'stick to the road, round the church and in at the front.'

Where the lane began to go uphill, it forked. Jack, looking to the left to see where it led, glimpsed cottages, a mail box in a stone wall and another flash of red that could be a telephone box, one of the old kind. He said nothing. If he pointed it out, Dad might prefer to use it and they would not go back to the manor.

From the road the house looked inviting beyond its double gates, with the bare beech trees and dark evergreens behind it, the chill gardens all around and the warm lights in the downstairs windows. From one of the upstairs windows an arm was waving.

'Someone's pleased to see us,' Dad said, 'unless of course they are waving for help.'

'That's Julius,' Jack said, waving back, and walked through the gates with new confidence.

'Who's Julius?'

'He lives here. We think we're second cousins.'

Dad did not ask how they had managed to meet. He had stopped in the gateway and was staring at the house. 'Imagine being able to call this your home and knowing that you'd got to leave it. Steve was saying that it's going into the estate.'

So Dad and Steve had at least spoken to each other. 'What does that mean?'

'The old man's will – it was badly worded. Everything's being sold up and the proceeds shared among his surviving children, only there may not be any. My father hasn't been heard of for thirty years, and there was an aunt who went to America and was never seen again. If she's still alive she may get the lot, which wasn't at all what Grandad intended. I think he wanted to avoid a row, but that's partly what the row's about. The lawyers are going to have a field day.'

The front door opened and Julius leaned out. 'Have you come back to say goodbye? Sudden twinge of conscience, what?'

'Actually, we wondered if we could use your phone,' Dad said. 'The car's packed up.'

Jilly appeared behind Julius. 'Of course you can. Where are the rest of you?'

'In the car.'

'Staying out of the way?' Jilly did not seem to be altogether joking. She looked pale and her eyes were still red-rimmed. She kept touching her temple with two fingers, the way people do who know they have a headache coming on, or hope that one is fading.

'We didn't think you'd want us all traipsing back.'

'That was tactful, but almost everyone has gone. A whole bunch swep' out in a tantrum just now. It was my fault, but what could I do?'

'Just a quick phone call and we'll be gone.'

'I doubt it. You won't get anyone out in a hurry on a day like this. Make your call and then you can all wait here and help us finish the leftovers. People were too busy fighting to eat.'

'We'll fetch them,' Julius said, leaping down the steps and grabbing Jack as he landed. 'We'll drag them back.'

'Don't you think your lungs have been exposed enough –'

Julius barked like a performing seal, on cue. 'Don't fuss, dear. I'm just faking now, for sympathy.'

Jilly threw him a coat. 'Be quick. It's foul out and getting fouler.' She seemed to know better than to argue with her son.

'We'll cut through the churchyard,' Julius said. 'The mob will have got clear.'

'We saw them as we came past. That's why we went round by the road.'

'Good thinking. Steve said they'd be a wild bunch. I thought it would be funny, but it wasn't. One of the All Blacks wanted to take away something as a keepsake, only it wasn't small, it was a wicked great ugly silver thing with knobs on, and Jilly said no, better not; I mean, she was very polite, but then they all turned on her and someone said they hoped there was an inventory because otherwise who'd be able to tell what *we'd* taken? They were all on about that, and watching each other to make sure that nobody else took anything. And this woman kept saying that GG had promised her the silver thing, and then they all started picking stuff up and arguing. GG had promised something to everyone, but it was all the same things.'

In the lane they had to press up against the hedge as, one after another, a BMW, a Peugeot and a Range Rover slewed out into the roadway and roared furiously towards the bend by the church.

'Let's hope they hit something,' Julius said. 'Let's hope they hit each other. No, don't let's hope that; they'd all come back to the house and wait while the breakdown people arrived.'

'Like us,' Jack said.

'Oh, no, not like you. When you and your father came in at the gate Steve said, "Oh, God, they're starting to come back again, let's hide," and Jilly said, "No, it's all right, it's the nice ones."'

'She said that?' Jack knew that he sounded as suspicious as he felt, but he would not have blamed Julius's family for hiding.

'Yes, she really did. She noticed you all because of your sister – her hair. And your parents were trying to be friendly. Anyway,' Julius said, 'I told them you were cool. So why did you sneak off?'

'Why do you think? Dad wanted to go before Auntie Bat got hold of us. I couldn't find you to say goodbye.'

'Auntie Bat? I'll tell Jilly that.' Julius smiled, which

33

made him look almost young. 'Hey, is that your car? There's no one in it.'

'Probably gone to the loo behind the hedge,' Jack said. 'There were queues at yours.'

'And Auntie Bat counting the bog rolls, I bet. No, it's all steamed up. There's someone inside.'

Jack tried the door handles. 'It's locked.' It was crazy to be alarmed, but out here, miles from anywhere in hostile territory, who knew what might not have happened?

A rear door opened and Marty looked out. 'It's OK, little bro, we're in the back, crouched out of sight.' She climbed out and Mum emerged behind her.

'Range Rover with bull-bars shunted Peugeot. More than words were exchanged. As potential witnesses we decided we weren't here.'

'I'm Julius. Jilly says please come back to the house and keep warm till the AA gets here. It's safe now, there's hardly anyone left.'

'Jilly? Your mother? Our hostess? Are your sure? She must have had enough for one day. We'll be all right here.'

'No, *please*, she'd be upset if you didn't. She'd come out with coffee and sandwiches. She would, she's like that. So it would be better for her if you came back.' Julius let rip with one of his death rattles. 'And better for me, of course. My weak chest . . .'

'I'm going,' Marty said. 'Come on, Mum. We can help clear up.'

They locked the car and went back down the lane. Even the Cavalier had gone. Theirs was the only vehicle left, perched forlornly at the top of the hill.

34

'Looks like everyone's gone,' Mum said hopefully.

'Auntie Bat's got a hired car coming from Oxford,' Julius said. 'And there were two other All Blacks who Eurotunnelled from Belgium and stayed overnight, but they've probably gone by now. I hope.'

'Did you say Auntie Bat?' Marty asked. 'The one who looks like a ferret crossed with a cactus? How very suitable.'

'Do you want to see over the house?' Julius asked. Mum and Dad and Marty were sitting round the fire with Jilly and Steve, and several bottles – for medicinal purposes, Steve said. Dad was virtuously drinking coffee because he had to drive.

'Where's Auntie Bat?' Jack said, as they slithered into the corridor with a plateful of sandwiches.

'Going round with a clipboard, making lists,' Julius said. 'Evil old hag. She's got everyone thinking that Jilly and Steve only looked after G G for his money. Well, they probably thought that in any case, but now they're all *saying* it. And it's not true. They'll just get a share of what's left when everything's sold – and you've seen how many they'll have to share it with.'

'There isn't a secret will or anything, is there?' Jack said. Stoke Crowell Manor had the look of a house where secret wills were discovered, sealed into forgotten cupboards behind the wallpaper. 'He might have left the house to you after all. You don't want to move, do you? Not from somewhere like this?'

'Of course we don't.' Julius reached the head of the stairs and peered round cautiously in case Auntie Bat were anywhere about. 'But we've always known that we'd have to. Granny looked after G G till she died, and then Jilly and Steve took over. We've got our own house, only someone's renting it. It's a pity, but it's quite fair. This is my room.'

The door was ajar. Julius pushed it open and inside stood Auntie Bat, with her clipboard. She must have heard them coming and Jack thought that she might at least have looked guilty, but she glared at them as though they were the trespassers.

'Everything in here's mine,' Julius said, dangerously close to losing his cool. His voice shook. 'Everything. The books are mine. The desk's mine. The bed's mine. We brought it all with us from Banbury.' Auntie Bat continued to stare. 'And the carpet. And the rubbish in the wastepaper basket.' He strode across the room, picked up the basket, which stood by a desk, and upended it in the middle of the floor. 'Look. All mine.'

Auntie Bat ignored the crackling heap of papers and fluff. 'The looking-glass?' It was a big oval one in a gilded frame, hanging above the mantelpiece. Julius flushed, slightly.

'N-no. That was already here.'

'The wardrobe?'

'No –'

Auntie Bat made a note on the clipboard. 'Yes,' she said, 'I see,' and walked out of the room without looking at either of them.

'Go and push her downstairs,' Jack suggested helpfully.

Julius shook his head and began to stuff the rubbish back into the wastepaper basket.

'I shouldn't have said it was all mine. Jilly told me to be careful of what I said. But none of it's hers either.'

'Do you think she's looking for a secret will?'

'Oh, belt up about secret wills, there isn't any secret will. Who do you think you are, the Famous Five? You're as bad as the rest of them.'

'I'm not,' Jack said. It was almost the worst insult he had ever heard. 'Sorry. It just seems so unfair.'

'Well, it's not as fair as GG meant it to be. He didn't realize what it would be like for us. He didn't realize much at all, in the end. I don't think he even knew who Jilly was.'

Jack looked out of the doorway. Auntie Bat was on the half-landing at the bend in the stairs, poking about in a little triangular cupboard hung in the angle of the walls.

'Even if she's not looking for a will,' he said, 'she seems to be looking for something.'

'What do you mean?' Julius pushed the basket back under his desk and sat in the middle of the carpet, as if he were waiting for it to take off. 'She's just making sure that she knows what's here so that we don't try to take anything. I wouldn't want that disgusting mirror anyway,' he added, 'or the wardrobe.'

'Good cover, though,' Jack said. 'She could be secretly searching while she was pretending to do the – the – what was it?'

'Inventory. You've got secrets on the brain. What could she be looking for?'

'The blood feud?' Jack said. 'I thought it was a joke till I saw them all. Can we look at the other rooms now she's gone downstairs?' He had been in Julius's room long enough to see that there was no computer, so they might as well go and look at something else.

Julius led the way along the landing, opening doors. 'Jilly and Steve's room, spare room, GG's room –'

'Did he die in there?' Jack said.

'Yes, but there's nothing to see. Look.' The room was big, with a table and easy chairs, like an ordinary sitting room, but at one end was a high bed with all the linen stripped off and the mattress exposed. The curtains were drawn right back and the dreary daylight filled the room unforgivingly.

'Did you see him?' Jack said.

'Who?'

'GG. Did you see him after he died?'

'I saw him in his coffin,' Julius said. 'I was staying with a friend the night he went. It was very quick.'

'What was it like?'

'He wasn't there,' Julius said. 'When I say he went – that's just it. It was his face, and his body, but there was no one there. Something had gone away – he'd gone away. It was the strangest thing . . .' he said, almost to himself.

Jack was looking out of a landing window, towards the road. He saw Dad crossing the gravel with a mechanic. They climbed into a yellow van parked by the gates and drove away. 'AA's here,' he said. 'We'll be going soon unless there's something really wrong. Is there anything else to see?'

'Not up here. There's the library. We can go down the back stairs to that.'

'A library? In a house?'

'Yes, like in whodunnits, *The Body in the Library*, you

know. But we only call it that for a joke, because this is the sort of house that *ought* to have a library. It's just the room where GG kept most of his books. We've put all of them in there now, ready for sorting out. Steve says no manor house is complete without a library.'

Unlike the wide shallow staircase at the other end of the house, with its polished banisters and turned newel posts, the back staircase was steep and boxed in, concealed top and bottom behind doors. The library was exactly opposite the lower door.

Apart from the long room with the log fire, this was the warmest part of the house.

'We've had to keep the heating on in here so that the books don't get damp,' Julius said. He sniffed. 'Eau-de-Mothball. Auntie Bat's been in here. Hah! Here's further evidence, as if I needed it.'

Jack had been imagining leather-bound volumes on oak shelves that stretched from floor to ceiling, but they were just ordinary books, in ordinary bookcases, the kind that they had at home. There was a table under the window and a sideboard along one wall. One of its two doors was open and it was at this that Julius was pointing.

'You said she was looking for something. She must have been disturbed before she could get in at the other end.'

'What's in there?'

'Only photograph albums. We have to keep the key turned or the doors swing open – like that one's doing.'

'It's empty.'

'The albums are at the other end. That better not

be empty –' Julius transferred the key to the lock in the far door and opened it. There were books stacked inside, bound in leather and cloth.

'Can we look?' Jack said.

'Sure.' Julius lifted them out, in two piles, and put them on the table. 'Some of this stuff's really historic.' He opened the topmost volume. 'This is the oldest. Steve says photography was in its infancy when these were taken.'

The photographs were portraits, of men with side-whiskers, women in ringlets and lace caps, scowling children in peculiar frocks that left their shoulders bare.

'They all look stuffed,' Jack said.

'That's because they had to sit still for so long,' Julius explained. 'They didn't have snapshots and the cameras were enormous. These pictures are 150 years old.'

Under each portrait names were written in tiny sloping handwriting as neat as print. *Harriet Stopford*; *Cousin Mary*; *Thomas Stopford*; *Thomas Wilson*; *William Jarvis*; *Ewart Rawnsley Stopford Gethin*; *Marguerite de la Salle Gethin*. Ewart Rawnsley Stopford Gethin was a very small child who had not understood about sitting still. He had three eyes.

'Are they all family – our ancestors?' Jack said. This morning he could have counted his relatives on the fingers of both hands. In the last few hours he had acquired twenty others and now here were hundreds more, all dead but curiously part of him and Julius. And Dad. But not of Mum and Marty. And yet, he thought, everyone in the world is on the end of something like this, even if they never knew about it, and he remembered the family tree that Julius had started to draw in the belfry of the church, during the funeral. He had been surprised then by the number of people whom Julius had known of and yet, compared with this lot, they were scarcely more than a bunch of twigs on the topmost branches.

'This one's more interesting,' Julius said, sliding an album out from the bottom of the pile. 'There are people we actually know in here – well, people we know *about*.'

There were dates in this album and although people were wearing old-fashioned clothes they did at least look alive. That is, they looked as if they had been alive when the photographs were taken.

'Here's GG in the Navy,' Julius said, pointing out a bearded man in a heavy coat. Underneath someone had written, *Robert, October 1941*. Jack examined him closely. This was the first time he had ever seen his great-grandfather. All around him, in the albums, were portraits of young men and women in uniform, Richard in the Army, Jeremy in the Army, Tom dressed for air raids in a tin hat, Dorothy in the WRNS, Pat nursing, John in the Boy Scouts.

Jack looked at Pat, a pretty girl with curly hair, smiling at the camera. He flipped back a few pages. There she was again, alone, with the others, with a cat, with a scooter, getting younger and younger; Patsy with Tom, Patsy with John, Patsy with Rover, Patsy roller-skating, skipping, on a bike. How had pretty Patsy become Auntie Bat?

Half-way through the next album the pictures stopped. After November 1948 there were no more.

One minute there they were, smiling, waving; the next, they had all vanished. The rest of the pages were blank. Was that the moment when the blood feud began?

He looked again at the last pages that lay empty, waiting for the photographs that were never taken. The pages were stiff black double sheets folded over, with slits ready-cut so that the photographs could be slotted in. He pressed the outer edge of one page and the two leaves parted. Something fell out. A photograph had by mistake been slipped inside the gap. It was nothing special, another baby, crouching among some leaves and banging a saucepan with a wooden spoon. In pencil, on the back, someone had scribbled *Stephen, 1951.*

'When was your dad born?' he said.

'1950,' Julius said. 'Why?'

'Is this him?'

'Might be. Where did you find it?'

'It was between the pages. All the other pictures stop at 1948.'

'I know. That must have been the start of the blood feud. Is there anything else in there?'

'Like a secret will?'

'Oh, give it a rest.' But it was a joke now. They both laughed. 'No, more photographs, I meant. How did you get it out?'

Jack showed the trick of pressing the edge of the double pages. They took an album each and began to work their way through.

'Don't try it with the older ones,' Julius warned, 'they aren't made the same way. The pictures are meant to be mounted between the pages. There's holes cut out to make frames.'

Behind them the door opened.

'And what do you think you are doing with those?' a voice demanded. It was Auntie Bat.

Julius looked round.

'I'm just showing Jack the family photos.' Although he was telling the truth he sounded guilty. Jack did not look up and did not turn to face Auntie Bat. At the exact moment the door opened, his fingers, sliding between two leaves, had found something stiffer than the pages which concealed it. This was not one loose photograph, it was a flat packet; he could feel the edges of the paper folded round it.

Auntie Bat was coming into the room. More furtively than he would have thought possible, he slid the packet from between the pages, under the palm of his hand, and flicked it into his sleeve. As Auntie Bat reached him and looked over his shoulder, he raised his forearm and felt the packet slide down the sleeve into his elbow, where he clamped it against his chest.

'It's just old pictures. We were just looking.'

'Looking for what?' She plucked the album out of his hand and slammed it shut.

'Not for, at,' Julius said.

'They are not yours to look at,' Auntie Bat said, gathering the whole pile of albums together and trying to lift them.

'They're not yours either,' Julius said softly.

'These are mine,' Auntie Bat said. She was lying. She knew they knew that she was lying and stared at

43

them, daring them to challenge her. 'This is not your house and the contents are not yours. Now, go back to your parents.'

'Trouble?' Steve put his head round the door, sized up the situation, decided instantly that the best response would be to pretend that nothing was going on and said, 'I might have known that you'd be in the very last place I looked. Jack, the car's fixed and your parents want to get going as soon as possible. Do excuse us, Pat, we'll be back in a minute.' He held the door open for Jack and Julius and closed it firmly behind them before Auntie Bat could follow.

'She's after the albums,' Julius said.

'Well, she's not getting them, not yet anyway. No, don't bother to explain, you know I'd believe you above her any time. Of course you weren't doing anything wrong.'

Jack decided that now was not the time to confess that he had indeed done something wrong, or, at best, something that he ought not to have done.

At the foot of the main staircase Jilly, smiling and comforted, was helping Marty and Mum with their coats. They chatted like old friends, promising to get in touch soon.

'I'd ask you back tomorrow,' Jilly said, 'but – well – you see how things are.' She noticed Jack approaching. 'Oh, Jack, thank you for Auntie Bat. I'll think of that every time I see her. It will keep me sane.'

Dad was parking at the double gates. Jack went out and got into the back of the car with Marty. He rubbed a clear patch in the mist on the rear window and looked out as they drove away, so his last sight of the manor was Steve and Jilly waving from the front door. Julius loped across the gravel and into the road, where he stood waving with one hand and making cryptic signs with the other. He was evidently trying to tell Jack something, but it was hard to imagine what.

'That is one serious weirdo,' Marty said appreciatively.

'No, he's not,' Jack said, automatically contradicting her; privately he thought that she had a point.

'The family Brain,' Dad said. 'Steve thinks they should have put his name down for Mensa at birth, but apparently he was quite normal until he started reading – at age two and a half.'

No one said anything else for a long time. They were almost back at the motorway junction before Mum spoke at last: 'What an appalling crew they were. The only comfort is, we'll never have to see any of them again.'

'We'll see Steve and Jilly, won't we?' Marty looked up urgently, not even waiting for the end of a paragraph. 'And Superbrat.'

'Brat yourself,' Jack muttered, but he was wondering now what Julius had thought about *him*, blathering on about secret wills like some little kid. No wonder he had lost his temper.

'Oh, we'll definitely keep in touch with Steve and Jilly,' Mum was saying. 'How do they stand it? Sainthood's not good enough for those two.'

'There wasn't much to stand, up till now,' Dad said. 'Nobody went near them while the old man was alive. And nobody's actually got it in for them personally; they're just tearing each other to shreds.'

'But why?' Marty said. 'We still don't know why. It can't just be the aliens.'

'If you could face asking Auntie Bat,' Dad said, 'I think you might get the answer. Or there again, you probably wouldn't. But she knows what happened. She hasn't forgotten or forgiven.'

He and Mum began talking about the traffic and whether it would be wiser to risk driving back through London instead of round the M25. Marty returned to her book. Jack, recalling that he too had a book, took it out of his pocket. He knew that he would never be able to read it without feeling ill but he had to get rid of the contraband package that was still up his sleeve, the sharp corner digging into the soft flesh of his inner elbow. He straightened his arm and jerked it until the packet slid into his hand.

He glanced sidelong at Marty. She had just begun a new chapter. Mum and Dad were occupied. He opened the book and slid the packet inside. No one was paying any attention to him. He could take one quick look.

It was of about the same dimensions as a small postcard and four or five millimetres thick, wrapped in heavy white paper printed with some kind of pattern on one side. He flipped the folds apart. Inside was a sheaf of photographs, a dozen at least, all different sizes, but a quick look at the top one convinced him that whatever he had here it was best looked at in private, so he folded the paper back into place and closed the book over it.

The photograph showed a group of people pointing up into the air. It must have been taken around 100

46

years ago, for the two men had boaters and striped blazers; the women wore wide hats and long dresses with big puffed sleeves.

Which made it all the stranger that the thing they were pointing at, sailing over their heads, was a flying saucer.

Chapter Four

*I*n his bedroom he made ready to repel boarders.
There was no lock on the door and he could
hardly wedge a chair under the handle without
arousing suspicion. Damien Dudsworth had barri-
caded himself in his bedroom for a whole weekend after
a row with his mum, but Dudsworth was celebrated for
going OTT. All Jack needed was an early-warning
system. He compromised by poking the sleeve of his
jacket into the gap under the door. If someone opened
the door suddenly the coat would foul it and there
would just be a few words exchanged about his hanging
clothes on the floor. The loo would be the best place
but Dad was in there, reading.

Jack removed the white paper wrapping carefully
and refolded it along the creases. Then he cleared a
space on his desk and laid out the photographs. The
smallest was only a few centimetres square, the largest
– the flying-saucer one – was postcard-sized. They

were all old, but some seemed newer than others; in fact the flying-saucer picture was the oldest of the lot and it was the only one that looked at all interesting. Some of the others were close-ups of people and there were several landscapes with tiny figures in them, taken by someone who had no telephoto lens. But he had noticed that in the car and was ready with an old pair of Dad's reading glasses. The left lens was plain but the right was strong enough to use as a magnifier. He examined one of the landscapes through it. The little people developed faces, features: a man in a chequered pullover, plus fours and a huge flat cap, standing with a woman in a cloche hat and a low-waisted dress, with a pale shapeless blur hovering beside them that might, like three-eyed Ewart, have been a small child or a dog that moved. Another shot was of a small girl in a straw hat with rosebuds round it, holding a bunch of flowers and looking at – something, something with a large head and very small ears. He had been wrong. The photographs might not be interesting, but there was something strange about all of them, although nothing else so strange as a flying saucer. One showed woodland with a person – or was it a person? – half seen among tree trunks. Another little girl held out her hand to a faint fuzzy creature with what looked like wings. From among sun-dappled leaves an indistinct face looked out. The smallest picture seemed to have been taken at night, the silhouettes of leafless winter trees, but the sky was eerily lit up behind them as if by a floodlight.

He turned all the photographs over, tipping them with his fingernail so as not to mark them. There was nothing written on the backs. He looked again at the flying saucer and the four people running along, pointing. It was the clearest of the lot, a little faded but not even slightly blurred: the two women in their floppy hats, the men in their blazers and boaters and thick moustaches, and the spinning shape above their heads. How could he tell that it was spinning? It just seemed to have such energy, he could almost see it move, slightly tilted, with the dome just showing above the rim and – yes – that was what gave the illusion of speed, a slight darkness at one edge, like vapour.

Even under the lens it was no clearer and no less strange.

Then history repeated itself. He heard the door handle turn and, as fast as he had earlier that afternoon, when Auntie Bat surprised him in the library, he swiped the whole collection together and skimmed them under the duvet.

The sound of the handle was followed by a predictable cronking squeal as the door engaged with his jacket sleeve and strained the hinges.

'What are you playing at?' Marty demanded from outside.

'Sorry – I left my coat . . .' He swung round and twitched the jacket out of the way. Marty, who was still leaning on the door, fell into the room.

'Was that a booby trap?'

'Accident.' He hung his jacket on the hook behind the door.

'Pull the other one. What have you got stashed away? Substances? You're blushing. Girlie mags, I bet.'

'It was an *accident*.'

'You must have something to hide.'

'What are you doing in here anyway?'

'I came to tell you,' Marty said, looking injured, 'that there's someone on the phone for you.'

'Who?'

'I didn't ask. One of your lowlife mates from school, I expect. Creepy Crawford or Rukash the Roach.'

He went down to the phone in the hall. Marty hung around.

'Bog off,' Jack said. 'And don't listen on the extension. Hullo?'

'Jack?' He could not quite place the voice. 'It's Julius.'

'Oh. Hullo.' He was so startled that he could not think of anything to say.

'You still there?'

'Yes.'

'Alone?'

'Yes.' Marty had not picked up the extension.

'This could be the end of a beautiful friendship,' Julius said. 'I *was* hoping that you'd ring first.' There was a pause. 'You know what I'm talking about, don't you? Or have you sunk to the level of Auntie Bat?'

Jack was almost too ashamed to answer. He remembered Julius's manic contortions seen through the rear window. He had been miming a telephone call. Evidently the manor phones still had dials, not buttons. And in any case, Jack ought to have been in touch at once, as soon as he got home.

'I've only just had a chance to look; I didn't want the others to know yet. I've been trying to work out what it is.'

'So what is it?' Julius said. 'I saw you palm something when Auntie Bat came in. So I kept quiet. *And* I kept

51

quiet in front of Steve, in case he got the wrong idea. Or was it the right idea?'

'*No*. I never meant to nick anything, but I didn't want to let on to Auntie Bat that there was anything to nick. I didn't see what it was, I just felt it was there, and I was getting it out when the door opened. If she hadn't come in I wouldn't have hidden it, I'd have shown you. I wasn't hiding it from *you*.'

'OK, but look, what is it? Because you were right, Auntie Bat's got it into her head that something's missing, only she won't say what. She's just crashing around the house saying slanderous things to Jilly and Steve. Mostly she's in the library, worrying at the books.'

'It's photographs, that's all,' Jack said. 'I mean, they're a bit odd, but they're just photographs. There aren't any of *her*. They can't be what she's after.'

'I think it is,' Julius said, 'because she was just snouting about to start with, wasn't she? It was only after she caught us with the albums that she really lost her rag. She wants to take them away with her but Jilly put her foot down and there was the mother of all punch-ups out in the hall. They're still at it. I'm in the phone box round the corner, in the dark because the light bulb's blown. I had to dial you by *feel*, and I got three wrong numbers and I can't see how much time I've got left, so this call could end any second.'

'What's your number – I'll ring you back.'

'Can't see it, can I? Call me tomorrow at home, or I'll call you. The bat should have flown by then.'

'Are you going to tell Steve what I've got?'

'Not yet. But they'll have to be returned or –'

The phone went dead. Jack slowly replaced the handset and pictured Julius at the other end of the line, alone in the unlit telephone box in the deserted lane, in the foggy darkness 100 miles away, on the flank of those looming hills.

He went into the kitchen, where Dad was playing telly chefs with the microwave.

'Here's one I prepared earlier,' he said, whipping out something flat, yellow and bubbling, like a geological phenomenon. 'Are you joining us, Jack?'

'Who was that on the phone?' Mum asked as he sat down. While they were all here under his eye, there was no chance of anyone running upstairs to look under the duvet and find his hoard. Not that anyone would. Bed linen was changed on Fridays, he had done it himself this morning, and no one went into his room otherwise. But you could never tell for sure.

'I left my light on,' he said, leaping up again, hearing, as he headed for the door, Marty chanting, 'Girlie mags, girlie mags.'

It was terrible how having a secret made you so – well – secretive.

By the time he came down Mum had forgotten that she had asked him who was calling. He ate his cheese and seafood bake, silently cursing himself for not having been the first to ring, for not having rushed to the phone to tell Julius what it was that he had discovered, because he had never meant to hide it from Julius in the first place.

But then, in the first place, he had never really foreseen a future in which he and Julius would share secrets, or even speak to each other. He had not thought much about it at all, but it seemed so possible that Julius would turn out to be like one of those people you met on holiday, got on with really well, wanted as a friend for life and then never saw again and forgot about in a fortnight.

Which could be what would have happened, he knew, had he not at that precise moment found the package as Auntie Bat came into the library. A few minutes earlier and he would already have opened it and Julius would have been the one to hand it over or hide it. A few minutes later – no, with Auntie Bat in the room they would have left the albums and never found the package at all. But would Auntie Bat have found it? Would she have been looking for photographs if they had not given her the idea?

'That was Julius on the phone just now,' he said.

'Julius of the funeral from hell? What did he want?'

'Just to talk. Can I ring him tomorrow?'

'Cheap rate all weekend. Why not?' Mum said. 'I want to keep in touch with them anyway.'

Something made Jack glance at Dad and he saw how pleased he looked. It had not struck him before that Dad might be unhappy about a blood feud that had cost him most of his family, not through murder but through bad temper: a thermonuclear family.

Somewhere in the middle drawer of the dresser was a real magnifying glass, a big old heavy thing with a brass handle and rim. The lens was scuffed from years of being polished on sleeves, but it was stronger than Dad's glasses. He rummaged for it.

'What are you looking for?' It was Marty's turn to

wash up and she flicked his neck with a damp tea-towel, not out of malice but because she happened to be holding it and he happened to be there.

'Nothing.' He found the handle of the glass with his fingers and drew it out from the heap of old television licences, gas bills, beer mats, elastic bands, corks and candle ends. What was that dog collar doing in there? He had not yet seen Julius's kitchen but if the Stoke Crowell drawers and cupboards were anything like this, Auntie Bat must be having her work cut out.

'A magnifying glass? That's really pervy, using a magnifying glass on girlie mags.'

'I haven't got any girlie mags.'

'What do you want it for?'

If only he had not tried to jam the door. Marty had merely wanted to call him to the phone. Now she suspected, rightly, that he was hiding something.

'I want to find Stoke Crowell on the map,' he lied fluently. Secrecy sharpened your wits, obviously.

'What map?'

'The Ordnance Survey atlas.' She could not argue with that. The atlas was in the bookcase in the living room and the maps were on a scale of one inch to four miles. Apart from Marty with her 20/20 vision, they all needed lenses to read them in detail.

'It's out of date,' Marty said, but not suspiciously, just stating a fact.

'Stoke Crowell won't have moved, will it?' Jack said. 'All the roads round there have been the same for years, you could see.'

Now that he had mentioned it, he thought that he might as well find Julius's village on the map, and he took the atlas upstairs with him to look at first in case Marty became genuinely curious and came in to see.

He traced their route from the M25, along the M40, on to the B481, through the sudden knots and angles of minor roads and lanes that jived below the scarp slopes of the Chiltern Hills. He recognized the woods that clad them by the patches of green on the map but he had to search before Stoke Crowell loomed into focus beneath the lens. It was such a small place that he could identify the separate black dots that lay round the loop of the road. That one was the manor, that was the church, right in the loop, and that must be the place with the telephone box outside, where Julius had made his call. Now that he knew exactly where to picture Julius, he turned back to the photographs, but even under the stronger lens he could scarcely make out more than he had already discovered. The man, the woman and the blob had, by their clothes, been photographed in the 1920s, but it was impossible even to guess at the rest. You could not tell when a *place* had been photographed unless you were old enough to remember how and when it had changed since. He had no idea where any of these places were, although for all he knew someone else might recognize them, Julius for instance. But one wood looked very like another, grass was grass and in these faded black and white and sepia prints – he knew that that brown tint was called sepia – even one face looked very like another. The two moustached men in the flying-saucer picture might have been twins.

Tomorrow he would tell Julius all about it, which would make him feel less of a toad for having taken the things in the first place, and then he might find out if they really had, by accident, stumbled upon the very thing that Auntie Bat had been searching for so anxiously.

Anxious was not quite the right word, he thought later, lying in bed and watching the moon slide past the window. Frantic was nearer the mark. How could anyone get so worked up about a few bad photographs? They weren't the kind of photographs that appeared in the tabloids, taken on the sly with a telephoto lens to ruin someone's reputation or wreck his family. They clearly had not been taken on the sly; at least one of them had been posed. But they had certainly wrecked a family.

No, he thought, we're on the wrong track. They aren't what Auntie Bat was looking for. They never started the blood feud.

Then what . . . ? He fell asleep wondering.

The snow was back in the morning, thin hard flakes that clicked on the last leaves of the rose bushes and stung his face when he went out to refill the bird-feeder. He had the place to himself. Marty was at a friend's house doing revision. Mum and Dad had gone to B&Q for timber, to continue the ongoing drama of the loft conversion. He made coffee, collected the photographs, looked up the number where Dad had already written it on the personal page in the directory and dialled Stoke Crowell Manor.

The phone was answered after only one ring, by Julius.

'Jack?'

'Yes.'

'I was waiting to pounce.'

'Can anyone hear you? Is there an extension?'

'Three,' Julius said, 'but we don't eavesdrop on each other. Go on, what have you got?'

'Look, really, it's just a bunch of photographs, but they are a bit odd. And one of them's really odd.'

'OK, now I'll tell you what I've found, or rather what I haven't found. Auntie Bat didn't go till last night. She's staying in a hotel in Oxford and she hung on till she *had* to go. Anyway, when she did go I went and had another look at the photograph albums. That was the row I was telling you about last night. She wanted to take them with her and Jilly said no, better not, and *she* said they were personal property and surely Jilly wasn't going to stop them all having keepsakes, and Jilly said what about the epergne – that was the thing with knobs on – we couldn't let anything go yet. *She* was getting suspicious by then, Jilly was, so when Auntie finally went, Steve said we'd better go through the albums to see if there was anything stashed away – no, I didn't tell him about you because you'd already said it was only more photographs.

'Anyway, we got the albums out, and some more booze, and Jilly and Steve got stewed, and I don't blame them after what they'd had to put up with. I showed them the picture you found of the infant Steve and then we went through the albums doing what you and I did, looking between the pages and – I'm not sure I should tell you this – Jilly said maybe we'd find a secret will.'

'Didn't you look at the photographs? They might have had clues.'

'There's thousands of them; you saw, didn't you? We didn't study them. We had a good look at the really old stuff because it might actually be quite valuable to a collector, but once it got to the snapshots and the hand-held cameras, we just skimmed the pictures and snooped between the pages. And the last one was just single pages anyway; the snaps were stuck in with mounts.'

'No,' Jack said, 'remember, the very last one had double pages, because that's where I found the picture of Steve as a baby, and . . . the others. It *was* the last, I remember, because it was the one that was only half full. That stopped in 1948.'

'Ah, there *is* another one. You hadn't got as far as looking at it, that's all. But the only people in it are GG and Great-Grandma, and Richard – that's my grandfather, their son, Steve's father – and my grandmother, and Steve and Jilly and me. It's the post-feud album. There's no one else in it at all.'

'Is that what you *didn't* find?'

'No, but I'd spotted something. After Jilly and Steve reeled off to bed – and they're still there, sleeping it off – I went back with my clear head and had another snout through. Some of the photos are missing.'

'People often take photos out of albums,' Jack said. 'Then they lose them or forget to put them back.'

'Yes, well, I expect I'd have thought so, but I'd already spoken to you by then and I knew what it was you'd found. How many, by the way?'

'Sixteen.'

'There's sixteen gaps. You remember most of them had writing underneath, you know, "Cousin George at Scarborough, 1932", that sort of thing. Well, I started looking at the writing under the ones that were missing.'

'What did it say?'

'Aha. I'm going to keep you in suspense and tell you the best one last. I wrote them all down this morning. Isn't strong drink a wonderful thing? Jilly and Steve will be out of it for hours. If they'd been on E they'd still be jumping about. Right, the most recent one was "Elsie, Wychwood, July 1938". Have you got a picture that might fit?'

'Elsie Wychwood?'

'Wychwood is a place, in the Cotswolds. It's a wood.'

'Oh, right. Well, there's one –' he shuffled the pack on the floor – 'one of a woman, what might be a woman, behind what might be a tree. Actually, it's hard to see where the tree ends and she starts.'

'OK, what about "Robert, Nellie and Angus, Edgebury Castle, 1929"? Robert and Nellie are GG and Great-Grandma.'

'There's two people in a field with a sort of blob beside them. It looks like the 1920s – well, *they* do. The field just looks like a field. There isn't a castle in it, just a sort of ditch. Who was Angus? Could he be the blob?'

'Does it look human?'

'Not really.'

'Might be a dog, then.'

'Maybe we've got blobs in the family. Perhaps that's the ghastly secret and Auntie Bat's been trying to hush it up.'

'"1936, Ju-ju with Olive and flowers".'

'There's a little girl holding flowers and looking at this thing with a big head. Maybe that's the olive.'

'Or the ju-ju. Next, "1923, Elsie and Fairies ha! ha!"'

'It says "ha! ha!"?'

'Yes, printed. Well, are there fairies? Come on, make with the gauzy wings.'

'There's something, but I can't see what. I looked under a magnifying glass too. It's a white shape, in a bush . . . *might* have wings . . .'

'Hm. Right, now, this is the one that ought to confirm my suspicions one way or the other,' Julius said. 'Is there one that is really odd?'

'I told you that.'

'Do you still think it's odd? Now that you know what was written under the others.'

'If my picture matches your caption, yes. It is still odd.'

'What is it?'

'Well, it looks,' said Jack, 'like four people, sort of old-fashioned, running across a field and pointing at a flying saucer.'

He waited for a gasp of amazement to come down the line, but Julius simply said triumphantly, 'How about this, then? "Alfred, Cecil, Maud, Josephine and unidentified flying object, Edgebury Castle, August 1910".'

Chapter Five

After a long pause Jack said, 'There weren't any UFOs in 1910.'

'There were at Edgebury Castle.'

'Where is Edgebury Castle?'

'I don't know. A lot of the captions mention it, like that one with GG and Nellie and the Blob.'

'But there's no castle in the picture. Or in the UFO one. There's no castles in any of them.'

'Anyway,' Julius said, 'we don't know that there were no UFOs in 1910, it's just that nobody photographed them, or else they didn't realize what they'd seen.'

'Whoever took this one knew what it was. Funny, though, sticking it away in an album and never saying anything about it. Wait a minute, Dad said something about somebody seeing aliens. He thought that was what the blood feud was about. I thought he was joking.'

'I dunno,' Julius said. 'People with theories can get really ferocious. Look at the cereologists.'

'The what?'

'The people who think crop circles are made by extraterrestrial life forms. They're all in rival societies, publishing rival magazines and rubbishing each other's ideas. I don't know what happened with our lot, but we haven't really got started yet. We have to reunite the photos with the albums, first off.'

'I can post them,' Jack said. 'Registered mail.' He thought of the cost.

'Don't do that. Come with them.'

'I'd be too heavy. Parcelforce for me.'

'I mean,' Julius said patiently, 'bring them. Come for a visit.'

'But it's miles.'

'Can't be that far,' Julius said. 'You got here and back yesterday. Where do you live? I've only got your phone code.'

'Sittingbourne. In Kent. We're on the Medway Estuary.'

'Have you got a station? Where do the trains get in to London?'

'Victoria, I think.'

'Easy, then. You can get a coach the rest of the way to Oxford or Abingdon. We'll pick you up. Would you be allowed to come?'

'I might. What about Steve and Jilly? Won't I be in the way?' Jack recalled how well the parents had got on yesterday, how happy Dad had been last night when Mum said that she wanted to keep in touch. He also recalled what was currently going on at the manor.

'They don't mind who *I* have over; we shan't get in

their hair. They'll be pleased.' Julius hesitated. 'Look, sooner or later they'll have to know about the photographs – the ones you've got. But not yet,' he added decisively. 'We can make up some sort of a cover story later. They're bound to be relieved that you got them out of the house before Auntie Bat found them, if they turn out to be a clue to the dread secret. You haven't shown anyone at your end, have you?'

'No, but they'll probably want to know too.'

'If we find out what's been going on, everyone will,' Julius said. 'But it's between us at the moment. I'm going to give Steve and Jilly till lunch-time and then wake them soothingly with black coffee. When the time's right I'll say that you and I want to get together again at once. You crawl around your parents and I'll ring this evening – no, I'll ask Steve to; make it official and responsible. It's a pity you can't come for Christmas.'

'Better not.' Supposing he and Julius discovered that on closer acquaintance they could not stand each other? 'They'd be a bit upset here if I suddenly took off. We like Christmas.'

'Don't you just sit around and watch videos and stuff your faces?'

'No, we don't. Do you?'

'No, but that's how it looks on telly. We've always had to be quiet because of G G. I thought we must be the only people in the world who didn't spend Christmas playing war games and watching violent films and grossing out with six-packs and deep-pan gunk. Oh, what a shame. I was quite looking forward to getting degenerate this year.' Then he said uncertainly, 'You do want to come, don't you?'

'Yes. Yes, I do.'

'Fast work,' Marty said. 'Youngest Aylward sprogs heal old wounds, diddle-diddle-plonk.' She played air harp and rolled her eyes upwards.

'I suppose you and Julius fixed this up between you,' Mum said. 'It's a pity you didn't meet sooner.'

'Well, we couldn't have, could we?' Jack was wondering what would have happened if they had met sooner. They might have disliked each other on sight. After all, they had not had much to talk about at the funeral. It was only after the scene in the bedroom with Auntie Bat that they had found themselves joining forces. And Julius was older, at least a year older. Once that would have made an enormous difference.

'Easy enough journey if you don't mind travelling alone,' Dad said, 'but with the roads the state they're in you'd better go the whole way by train.'

'Dodgy,' Marty said. 'Snow on the line, leaves on the line, frozen diesel, *corpse* on the line –'

'True, but train drivers don't suffer from motorway madness,' Mum said. 'Anyway, I sorted it out with Jilly. You get the 9.15 to Victoria, Circle Line to Paddington and catch –'

'He'll catch the wrong train,' Marty intoned.

'No, he won't. You catch the Bristol train to Didcot and Jilly will be there to meet you with Julius. We'll get you a ticket that lets you come back when you like, but I'd prefer you to be home before Friday.'

Jack knew that under any other circumstances Mum

would have made the same objections as Marty, but Dad wanted to keep the lines of communication open, not just because he liked Jilly and Steve but because he wanted his relatives back.

Ha, little did they know! On the other hand, they had seen the relatives at the funeral. Did he really want *them* back?

Jack made an early start on Monday, carefully timed for the first off-peak train, which was packed with Christmas shoppers. The Underground was crowded too and Paddington was daunting, until he realized that there were more people leaving the station than entering it. An InterCity train was unloading as he arrived. When the crowds cleared he located his train on the destination board, rang home to say that everything was running to schedule and went to find himself a seat.

The train followed the River Thames, bridging it several times. When they reached Reading it was on the right, then the track ran among the hills, the river reappeared in a curve on the left and the track crossed it again. It was a fast train, the stations swiped past. Suppose he had made a mistake and the train did not stop at Didcot; would he be stuck on it till they reached Bristol? But his ticket was checked, the inspector did not say 'You are on the wrong train,' and then the steep downland was behind them, a gently curving hill swelled by the track, beyond it another lower hill that seemed to have one tree on top, and in the far distance twin hills each crowned with a grove of trees.

All the snow had melted again and the bare landscape seemed almost transparent in the misty sunshine. It looked cold. How could sunshine look cold?

There were houses on either side of the track now, new red-brick estates, signs of a town; the train was sliding into a station and he saw the sign for Didcot Parkway first of all, then Julius, who had been at the very end of the platform, running alongside the train.

'I'm in a manic phase,' Julius said, as he climbed down. 'I am dispersing reserves of violently restless energy. Jilly's in the car park, so she'll have seen the train come in and there can be no hanging around. We've got about two minutes before she starts to wonder where we are, so have you remembered the photos or do I have to kill you now? Actually, I'll wait until everyone's gone and then strangle you in the subway.'

'Don't bother. They're here – on my person.' He tapped his inside pocket.

'Let's have a look – no. No!' Julius slapped himself on the head. 'Down, boy. Down. I'll be patient. We'll look at them properly when we get home. I haven't told anybody. Have you?'

'Not a word.'

Jilly was in the booking hall buying take-away coffees. 'Look, they make them with these clever flaps now, so you can drink without taking the lid off. We'll slurp as we drive along. Hullo, Jack, nice to see you again so soon, really nice.'

Jilly, in a woolly hat and thick sweater, rosy with the cold and smiling, looked so different that Jack only then realized how rotten she must have been feeling on Friday. She swung the car, a Vauxhall, out of the station forecourt and took it very fast along a road that led eastwards and had a view of the twin, mysterious hills. Jack sat with Julius in the back. 'What are those hills?' he said, as he saw them more clearly. 'I noticed them on the train.'

'Wittenham Clumps. There's an earthwork on top of one and a sort of witches' grove and a beech tree with ancient writing carved on it. They're part of the Sinodun Hills.'

The car drove through a small town, crossed the river, which must be the Thames again, Jack guessed, and began to climb. Suddenly he knew where he was: looking back through the rear window, he saw a view of the power station that he recognized, and then the car was on its way down the lane to the churchyard where, among the dark stone graves and darker yews, a bright heap of flowers showed where Great-Grandad was buried.

They left Jack's bag in the hall at the foot of the stairs and went into the kitchen.

'I'll leave you to forage,' Jilly said. 'There's plenty to sustain yourselves on. Sorry to rush off again but I've got an appointment with the solicitor in Abingdon at two. I'll see you later. If you do go out, leave a message, Julius. The answering machine's already on.'

She was gone again. Jack started to take the photographs out of his pocket.

'No, wait,' Julius said. 'Let's eat first, and *fast*, and wash our hands thoroughly before we start.'

'Don't you want to just look?'

'Of course I do, but we mustn't damage anything. And once we start looking we won't want to stop and

68

eat, and I'm hungry; aren't you? Let's be meticulous.'

They meticulously tore a loaf in half, slapped butter on the raw edges and ate it with cheese, standing up at the table and taking turns to swig at a two-litre bottle of cola. The kitchen was big, with a low ceiling and stone-flagged floor, like the hall, but it was fitted with very up-to-date appliances, excepting one gap for the fireplace, whose stone chimney breast went right up to the ceiling. It was lined with blackened bricks and from the beam across it old iron and copper pots hung on hooks. The fireplace itself, however, was occupied by a gas central-heating boiler.

'Right,' Julius said as they finished eating simultaneously, 'unpack later. Now, wash hands with mild green Fairy Liquid to remove grease without damaging our silky skin, and on with the chase. Owing to my forethought, there is no washing up.' As Jack scrubbed his fingers, Julius brushed all the crumbs off the table into his cupped hands and threw them in the pedal bin. 'The albums are still in the library but I've put them in chronological order – the ones we're interested in.'

In the library the albums were now on the table under the window. There were eleven of them, stacked in two piles, and four more laid out separately.

'These are the ones with gaps in,' Julius said. 'The others may turn out to be important, but we'll start with what we know about. Let's have the photographs.'

Jack drew the envelope from his pocket and handed it over. It seemed only fair that Julius should be the one to open it.

'Is this what they were in?'

'No, it was a bit of wrapping paper. I thought they'd be safer in this.'

'Might have been a clue,' Julius said, frowning.

'I'll find it when I go back. Mum won't be in my room again until Friday and she'd never throw anything away without asking. Anyway, there wasn't anything special about it, just some kind of pattern.'

'What kind of a pattern?'

'Black and white. I didn't really notice.'

Julius was looking at the photographs. He had spread them out on the table in a row and stared at them before saying anything.

'Tell you what,' he said at last, 'they're bad.'

'Bad bad or bad fabulous?'

'Bad as in terrible. They're crap photographs.'

'Except the UFO one.'

'No, that's almost suspiciously good, isn't it? I'm surprised they kept any of the others. You wouldn't think they were worth putting in an album.'

'Are they the ones that are missing? Do they fit?'

Julius reached for the album on the left and opened it at a page where there were four pictures on one side and only three on the other. Where the eighth ought to have been was an empty frame. He lifted the UFO picture by its edges and slid it under the page, which, Jack could see, had once been pasted down. It fitted the frame exactly. The words underneath read *Alfred, Cecil, Maud, Josephine and unidentified flying object, Edgebury Castle, August 1910.*

'That must be it,' Jack said. 'That must be where it came from.'

'Here they are again,' Julius said, indicating the

other pictures. 'Look, *Cecil and Josephine, Edgebury Castle, August 1910; Maud and Alfred, Edgebury Castle, August 1910; Maud and Josephine, Clifton Hampden, August 1910; Cecil at Goring Lock, August 1910.*'

'What about the rest?'

Julius picked up another album. 'This'll be the one with the Blob, I think. *Robert, Nellie and Angus, Edgebury Castle, 1929.* Where's the picture?'

Jack pointed it out. 'It's only a little one.'

'It's only a little space.' He found the right page. 'It was fixed in with mounts originally; you can see where the sticky stuff was. Does it fit?'

'Exactly. Who – what do you think Angus is?'

Julius bent low over the album. 'If it didn't have a name, I'd say it was a trick of the light. Its feet don't touch the ground.'

'Is there an Angus in any of the other albums?'

'I haven't looked yet. It *could* be a dog – jumping up.'

'He isn't very big.'

'Lots of dogs aren't very big. He might be one of those white Scottish terriers. Where's the Olive?'

'The what?'

'You said you had one of someone with a big head.' Julius turned the pages of the third album until he came to another gap. *Ju-ju with Olive and flowers, May 1936.*

'This one.' They laid it in the space. 'Which is the Olive and which is Ju-ju?'

'The flowers came out quite well,' Julius said. 'Here's Maud again, in 1937, much older.'

'Well, she would be, wouldn't she?' Jack said.

'Twenty-seven years older. What about the Olive?'

'Pity you can only see its head.'

'Here's Elsie, Wychwood, 1938. No head at all and only one leg. Where's she fit?'

Julius opened the fourth album. 'Here – yes – perfect. This one's still got the mounts in.'

The writing under these photographs was all in different hands. Jack read the caption aloud: '*Elsie, Wychwood, 27 July 1938*. I wish they'd put the days on the others. See, there's a whole lot of Wychwood pictures on this page and they were all taken on 27 July. Was the UFO one taken at the same time as the others?'

They went back to the first album and turned to the adventures of Alfred, Cecil, Maud and Josephine.

'They're all wearing the same clothes,' Jack said.

'I don't think people had as many clothes in those days.'

'They don't look poor.'

'No, but nobody changed their clothes so often.'

'They aren't all in the same place, though. Edgebury Castle, Goring, Clifton Hampden: where are they?'

'Clifton Hampden's not far from here, nor's Goring. You came through it on the train,' Julius said. 'They're villages on the Thames. Cecil and Co. were probably boating. You could easily row from Clifton Hampden to Goring and back in a day. And they were wearing boaters.'

'What about Edgebury Castle? If these pictures *were* taken on the same day, it must be near here. And it's in so many other pictures – but you said you'd never heard of it.'

'Just because I've never heard of it doesn't mean it isn't near here,' Julius said.

'It's hard to miss a castle.'

'Not if it's in ruins. Let's get a map.' Julius headed for the door. 'We haven't lived here all that long,' he said, pausing; 'only four years.' He went out and then his head reappeared round the door. 'Don't move anything while I'm gone.'

'I'll come with you if you don't trust me.'

'I didn't mean that. I just meant don't muddle things up. Look at what you like.'

Jack flipped through the three albums with the pictures of the smiling young girl who had grown up to be Auntie Bat. The last of those was the one that began in 1938 with Elsie at Wychwood and ended in September 1944 with Robert mowing the lawn, while Nellie stood holding a basket of apples that she was picking off a tree. *In the garden*, it said underneath, but there was no mystery about where the garden was. When Jack raised his eyes he could see it, the same view as in the photograph, for in the middle of both was the church tower. Even the apple tree was still there, although the yew hedge had grown taller. Whoever had taken the photograph had been standing on this very spot, shooting through the open window.

Julius came back with a map.

'Does that have castles on?'

'I don't know. They usually mark historic sites these days, but this is an old one of GG's, 1919.'

'Edgebury Castle doesn't look very historic, does it? There aren't even any ruins.'

'Perhaps the person who took the picture was standing in front of the ruins,' Julius said.

'You'd think they'd want them in the picture.'

'Maybe they weren't interesting ruins.'

'They weren't interesting in 1929 either, when Angus the Blob was there.'

'If it was a place they saw often, maybe they wouldn't bother to photograph it. I've seen people stop their cars and photograph this place,' Julius said, 'but we never do. Though I suppose we might now,' he added.

They found their stretch of the Thames Valley on the map and settled down to examine it, centimetre by centimetre.

'Here's Goring . . . Here's Clifton Hampden. You take the left bank and I'll take the right bank. Look for anything with Edgebury in its name – you know, Edgebury-on-Thames, Edgebury St Egbert, or something. And look for *any* castles,' Julius said. 'They might have had the name wrong, like called it Edgebury Castle when really it was, say, Frogshead Castle *near* Edgebury. Names change.'

'Old names don't,' Jack said. 'Dover Castle's always been Dover Castle.'

'The Romans didn't call it Dover. The Latin name is Dubris.'

'I don't think the Romans had a castle there.'

'They had a shore fort and a lighthouse. I've seen it, in the grounds of the castle. You ought to know, it's your stamping ground. Anyway, concentrate,' Julius said severely, as much to himself as to Jack.

'I wish maps had indexes,' Jack said, 'and I wish you had a magnifying glass.'

'There's one in the drawer of the table,' Julius said. 'Not a glass, one of those big flat Fresnel lenses. We can both look through it.' He fetched it and they resumed their scan.

'There's a castle here,' Jack said. 'Near the river – no, it's Castle Hill.'

'That's one of the Sinoduns. It's not called Edgebury.' Julius leaned across. 'What's that, there?'

'Lowbury Hill. They might have been on bikes instead,' Jack said.

'Who? Instead of what?'

'Alfred and Cecil and that lot. They might have been cycling, not in a boat. They might have had a car. They might not have been anywhere near the river between Clifton Hampden and Goring.'

'You're right,' Julius said, straightening up. 'And you're right about the index. We'll wait until Jilly gets back and borrow the road atlas. We can have put all this stuff away by then.'

'What about the loose photographs?'

'Keep them to ourselves for now,' Julius said, folding up the map regretfully. 'But there's definitely nowhere called Edgebury between here and Goring or Clifton Hampden.'

'Why here?'

'Well, they lived here,' Julius said. 'Maud was one of our great-great-aunts. Even if *she* didn't live here, one of them must have.'

Chapter Six

'*I* didn't have any great-aunts till last week,' Jack said. 'I mean, I didn't know that I had.'

'We knew they existed. We didn't know what they'd be like. But up till then I was like you. It was just me, Steve and Jilly, Great-Grandad – and Granny, but that was before we moved here.'

'Granny? GG's wife?'

'No, Steve's mother. She lived here and looked after GG until she died. She had a heart attack, she wasn't all that old. It was an awful shock; we used to see her all the time. After that Steve and Jilly decided to move here and look after GG.'

'And now you've got to go again?'

'Unless we find the secret will, you mean? You needn't worry about us,' Julius said. 'We've got a perfectly good house to go back to in Banbury. Steve teaches at the CFE. Someone's renting the house till the end of May, so if this place is sold before then *we'll* have to find somewhere to rent; that's the worst thing that can happen and it's not likely to. The housing market's very slow at the moment,' he added knowledgeably.

'Didn't your gran know what the dread secret was?' Jack said. 'Didn't Steve ever ask her?'

'Well, yes, he did,' Julius said, 'but she always claimed not to know, or not to know much.'

'What about her husband, Steve's dad?'

'Richard, G G's eldest son. He died years ago when Steve was quite small. He was in the Army – the regular Army. There's a picture of him somewhere, in his uniform.'

'In here,' Jack said, remembering. 'The album that ends in 1944 – and the half-empty one. They were all in uniform.'

'Everyone was,' Julius said. 'There was a war on. Here we are, *Richard, June 1945*.'

'He's your grandfather.'

'Was. Look, there's some evidence here, if you like. The blood feud or dread secret or whatever probably started in 1948, because after that there are no more albums with everyone in, just this one I was telling you about with *our* family in it. Now for some reason the family split, and this is *how* it split. G G, that's Robert, and Nellie, his wife, Richard and his wife, Edna; then later, Steve and his wife, Jilly, and me. O K ? Doesn't it look as if it might have been Richard who did – whatever was done?'

'Why Richard?'

'Because it was our lot who were being shunned and ostracized. Auntie Bat never had anything to do with

77

us and she was Richard's cousin. Dorothy and Jeremy – these two here – never showed up, and they were his brother and sister, and then there was his youngest brother, John.'

'*My* grandfather,' Jack said, looking at the Boy Scout. 'So who saw the aliens at the bottom of the garden?'

'Yes, what is this with the aliens?'

'I told you, that's what Dad said when we asked what the row had been about. He said one of his uncles had seen aliens at the bottom of the garden.'

'This garden?' Julius wondered, looking out of the window. 'Is *he* hushing something up?'

'No, he'd be dead keen on solving the mystery. But he thinks Uncle and the aliens *had* been hushed up and there was an almighty row – no, Mum said that. They don't know anything more than we do, less probably.'

'There's plenty of uncles to choose from,' Julius said. 'Let's do a proper family tree.'

'What about finding Edgebury Castle?'

'Edgebury Castle's a no-no at the moment,' Julius said.

'It needn't be. We've got an Ordnance Survey atlas at home. It's got an index. It even lists all the rivers and ancient monuments.'

'Are you going to nip home for it?' Julius asked heavily.

'No, but I'll ring and ask my sister to look it up.'

'Won't she ask questions?'

'She always does, but it doesn't matter, does it? She might even be able to help.'

Julius looked undecided. 'Don't tell her too much. I want . . .' He stopped. Jack understood. Julius really wanted to do the whole thing himself, without even Jack's help, and no doubt that was exactly what he would have been doing had it not been Jack who had found the packet of photographs. On the other hand, if Jack had not been there, being shown over the library, Julius might never have discovered what it was that Auntie Bat was looking for, and Auntie Bat might have found it.

'I'll lie,' Jack said, heading for the door. 'Which phone do I use?'

'Kitchen.' Julius had a drawer open under the table and was foraging among pens and papers.

The kitchen telephone hung on the wall. Jack dialled and prayed that Marty would be home. Dad or Mum would have checked out the atlas for him, but they would be at work.

'Hullo?' It was Marty.

'It's Jack.'

'Homesick already? Do you want us to come and fetch you?'

'Give it a rest,' Jack said. 'I've only been here an hour. I want you to look something up for us.'

'Yeah, dictionaries can be hell if you can't spell in the first place, looking up physics under f and psycho under s –'

'It's not a word, it's a place. Edgebury Castle. Can you look in the Ordnance Survey atlas?'

'What are you up to?'

'Nothing. It's just a place we want to know about.'

'After an hour? Why the rush?'

'No rush, we just haven't got the right sort of map here.'

'Do you want to hang on or shall I call back?'

Jack thought of the answering machine, waiting to trap their every word. 'I'll hang on. It won't take you a moment.'

While he waited he looked round the kitchen, at the sun shining on the stone floor and the sooty bricks in the chimney. It was so silent here. Even with the window slightly open he could hear no sound, although after he had listened for a moment or two he noticed that what had seemed like silence was actually resting on a continuous murmur that must be traffic, miles away on the M40. Marty's voice in his ear made him jump.

'No such place.'

'What?'

'No such place as Edgebury Castle. No such place as Edgebury anything, and no Great Edgeburys or Little Edgeburys, before you ask. I looked.'

'Not anywhere?'

'Not in the U K,' Marty said. 'Where did you think it might be?'

'Round here somewhere. Thames Valley.'

'Are you sure it's a castle?'

'Well, if it's *called* Edgebury Castle –'

'It might be a pub – *The* Edgebury Castle.'

'It would be named after a real one, though, wouldn't it? Pubs are always named after something.'

'Like the Edgebury Castle and Firkin? Castles fall down. It may not be there any more.'

'There'd be ruins.'

'Not on a map necessarily.'

'Stonehenge is on a map.'

'Stonehenge is still there.'

'Edgebury Castle was still there in 1910,' Jack said incautiously.

'Maybe it got bombed in World War Two. Sorry, can't think of anything else. Having a good time?'

'Great.'

'Solved the mystery yet?'

'Which mystery?' Jack said, guiltily innocent.

'Hah! Thought you were on to something,' Marty said gleefully and hung up.

Hoping that Marty was too busy to start making educated guesses, he went back to Julius in the library.

'Any luck?' Julius was being meticulous again with a ruler, drawing their family tree.

'No, she couldn't find it.' He looked over Julius's shoulder at the rows of names.

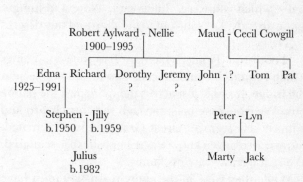

'Maud and Cecil, them in the photo? With the flying saucer? What about Josephine and Alfred?'

'I'm not sure where they belong,' Julius said.

'Cowgill.' Jack remembered hearing Cowgills

mentioned on Friday. 'Auntie Bat's a Cowgill. There's another lot . . . Ackroyds.'

'That's right. How did you know about them?'

'When we came to the funeral Mum was hoping people would be held up by the snow, the ones coming from the North. It was Cowgills and Ackroyds.'

'Maybe that's Josephine and Alfred, then, or their descendants.' Julius ruled his last line, and added their names in pencil. 'We'll have to get some more dates in later. In fact, when Jilly and Steve come home we'll confess everything and see if they can help fill in the gaps.'

'We'll tell them about the photographs then,' Jack said courageously, foreseeing that Jilly's warm welcome might cool off.

'We'll say you were getting them away from Auntie Bat – which you were,' Julius said. 'Now, I'm hungry again already. Let's slip out to the shop and buy desert.'

'Desert?'

'Tooth-rot. Things which are bad for you. Things which responsible middle-class parents do not keep in the fridge. It's only just across the road, past the phone box. We can come back through the churchyard and admire GG's grave. Great-Grandma was cremated. Steve doesn't even know where her ashes are scattered. We're a terribly careless family.'

While they were in the churchyard Jilly must have come home. They saw the Vauxhall parked on the gravel apron as they rounded the side of the house, but there was no sign of her. As they began to search, she looked out of the living room.

'There's an anonymous message on the machine,'

she said. 'I don't know who it's from or who it's for, only I suspect one of you two. A female voice, very cryptic.'

'What was it?' Jack said, immediately thinking of Marty.

'Play it, Sam,' Jilly said. 'The machine's in there.'

She held the door open for them and they went through. Julius pressed PLAY on the answering machine and Marty joined them in the long, quiet room.

'I've just thought, it may not be a real castle at all. Edgebury sounds like an earthwork to me. Think on.'

'What's that mean?' Jack said.

'Was that Marty? Smart lady,' Julius said. 'She could be right.'

'What does she mean, earthwork?'

'Like I was telling you, at Wittenham Clumps. That one's on Castle Hill, isn't it? They're usually Iron Age and they're often called Somethingbury; fortifications like Segsbury, Danebury, Cadbury – that's meant to be King Arthur's Camelot – and Silbury – that's an enormous man-made hill.' Julius beamed. 'I'm sure she's right. Edgebury *sounds* like an earthwork.'

'Does it? It still isn't on the map. When I rang her up she said there were no Edgeburys at all, not even like Great Edgebury.'

'We'll have to think about this,' Julius said. 'If it's a small place it might not be on a map like this. We'll have to look on one with Roman remains.'

'I thought you said Iron Age.'

'Well, *ancient* things, anything in Gothic print. There's a place near Princes Risborough called Cymbeline's

83

Mount. Cymbeline may never have existed, although he's supposed to have been King of Britain, but the mount is real. It's an old motte and bailey, a castle mound. There's one in Oxford.'

'And Canterbury. I know what you mean.'

'Right, well, Edgebury Castle may have been like that. You never see Cymbeline's Mount *named* on maps, you just have to know it's there.'

'Who was the mysterious female?' Jilly said, coming in, 'or shouldn't I ask?'

'Marty, my sister,'

'Have I heard of Edgebury?' Jilly said. 'It sounds familiar.'

'It's one of the places in the photograph albums, Edgebury Castle,' Julius said. 'We were trying to find out about it because you'd think a castle would be famous and we had never heard of it.'

'And Marty thinks it may be an earthwork? I came in to see if you wanted tea, coffee or light refreshments, but perhaps you've got something to tell me?'

'Why do you think that?' Julius said casually, but managing all the same to let his mother know that she was right.

'Because I've been into the library and the albums are not quite where they were last time I saw them. Not that there's any reason why you shouldn't look through them, but if you know something I don't, you might share it.'

'A-a-a-a-actually,' Julius said, 'we do know something you don't and we're going to share it when Steve gets home – aren't we?' he added, looking at Jack.

'Something I found,' Jack said, preparing to admit everything, but Jilly just said, 'Fair enough. I can wait.'

'So it's all right if we have another look through the albums?'

'Of course it is. Just don't take anything away.'

'She's going to be livid,' Jack said, as they went back to the library.

'No, she's not. Only people like Auntie Bat make her livid. But let's have another go at those photos. Lay them all out.'

They put the loose photographs in a row on the table. Julius studied them, frowning.

'Find the page where the flying saucer comes from – it's the brownish album with *Sunny Memories* on the cover.' Jack opened it at the place where there were seven photographs and one gap.

'Here we go,' Julius said. 'One day in August 1910, Maud Aylward, GG's sister, goes out for a row, or a bike ride or a picnic, with Cecil Cowgill, who's her fiancé, and Josephine and Alfred. They go – let's say they go to Clifton Hampden and they take a picture of Maud and Josephine. Then they go to Goring and they take a picture of Cecil in a rowing boat.'

'Maybe it was the other way round.'

'No, look at the shadows in this one. I think it was getting late when they took it. So they were heading downstream, Clifton Hampden to Goring. Somewhere in between they stopped at Edgebury Castle and . . . saw a flying saucer,' he finished lamely.

'If I'd seen a flying saucer I'd tell people about it,' Jack said. 'Do you think that was when they saw the aliens too?'

'Are you sure you'd tell people?' Julius said. 'What would they say? "Poor old Jack, seeing things. Touch of the sun." '

'I would if I'd got proof. That photo's proof, isn't it? And anyway, they didn't try to hide it, did they? They stuck it in the album with all the others, where anybody could see it.'

'Till someone took it out,' Julius said. 'Now, the next Edgebury picture is Nellie and Robert and Angus the Blob –'

'No, it's the next loose one. There are plenty of others still stuck in the albums.'

'Good thinking. You go on through that one, I'll start on this – and there's another that goes up to Christmas 1922. Put a slip of paper in at every Edgebury page. You can tear strips off this old exercise book – no, there's nothing in it, I looked.'

'No confessions of a teenage alien?'

They turned the pages in silence until Julius, laying aside one album and opening another, said, 'Found anything?'

'Sort of.' Jack riffled through the fringe of paper slips that was spraying out of the album. 'There's dozens of pictures taken at Edgebury Castle.'

'Same here. They must have spent half their time there.'

'Why? There's nothing there, except that ditch.'

'Which *may* be part of an earthwork. Everyone has a special place they like to go to. Or they just got into the habit because it was easy to get to. It must be close by.'

'Anyway, what I found,' Jack said. 'All the snaps still

in the albums are ordinary. They're just pictures of people standing around grinning. It's the odd ones that have been taken out.'

'That's what I noticed,' Julius said. 'You could understand somebody throwing them away because they were such bad pictures, but why keep them?'

'Can you see anything else in them that might tell us when they were taken? Like Didcot Power Station?'

'I keep wishing they'd built Didcot Power Station earlier. Every picture you take round here has got it belching steam in the background. One or two snaps have got trees in them – I think it's always the same trees because of the shape. They look the same even when they haven't got any leaves.'

'I suppose,' Jack said slowly, 'I suppose they weren't taken out because someone *thought* they were pictures of aliens?'

'What, Ju-ju and the Olive and Angus the Blob?'

'Well, they don't look human, do they?'

'The person who put them *in* the albums didn't think they were aliens. I don't think they had aliens in those days. Look, G G and Great-Grandma wouldn't have stood there posing with an alien beside them, would they?'

'Perhaps they didn't know it was there.'

'They'd have known once the picture was printed.'

'Perhaps they weren't the sort of people who thought there was anything odd in keeping a pet alien. I mean, they photographed a flying saucer and stuck it in the book. And what about that night-time shot of the trees. Is that supposed to be the saucer landing?'

'I think it's a German aircraft crashing during the war. There's one gap in the second-to-last album where the caption says *Hoist with his own petard*.'

'What's that mean?'

'Blown up with his own bomb,' Julius said. 'Is that Steve I hear, grinding over the gravel? He gets a lift down the M40 and cycles home from Stokenchurch. Yep, there he goes.'

Steve's bearded head glided past the window under a deerstalker hat with the flaps let down against the cold.

'In his Sherlock Holmes mode,' Julius said, 'which is all to the good. Steve's the great thinker in this family. We'll pick his brains in a bit. *Before* dinner, I think, because Jilly's roasting lamb in your honour and there will be red wine.'

'Does he always drink a lot?' Jack said. His own father seldom drank at all, but then, his job involved driving.

'I've given the wrong impression,' Julius said. 'The funeral was a special case. No, he'll just have a glass or two at dinner and a Scotch beforehand. We'll catch him over the Scotch, when his wits are sharpened, and before the wine, when they'll get ever so slightly blunt again.'

'I've finished this one,' Jack said. 'February 1918. Alfred and Josephine have disappeared. Cecil's lost an arm.'

'First World War,' Julius said. He opened the drawer under the table, took out the family tree and wrote *d. 1917?* by Alfred's name. 'We don't know about Josephine yet,' he said. 'She may have gone to the

Front as a nurse and got killed, or she may have just gone away grieving.'

'Was she a Cowgill or an Ackroyd? There must have been some Ackroyd relatives because there were Ackroyds at the funeral. Were they All Blacks or The Rest?'

'All Blacks were family,' Julius said. 'The Rest were people who knew us, or G G. Locals. *Normal* people. Now Robert – G G – got through World War One all right. I think Cecil died soon afterwards, but that was after Tom and Auntie Bat were born. Try this one next. I'm coming up to the end of 1922. In fact Auntie Bat has just made her first appearance, lying on a fur rug with nothing on. Yours begins in 1929.'

Jack tore up another handful of paper strips and opened the next album. There they all were again, the happy children: Patsy and Tom, Richard, Dorothy, Jeremy and John, the baby. Sometimes they had friends with them. Patsy was photographed with what seemed to be twin sisters, Olivia and Juliet Barnes.

'Hang about,' Jack said. 'Ju-ju and the Olive.'

'What about them?'

'They're people, Olivia and Juliet, two little girls. Twins, I think.'

'Not conjoined twins?' Julius said hopefully.

'No, well, they might have been once, but they aren't here. There's nothing strange about them at all.'

'No,' Julius said. 'The one where they look strange is the one that's been taken out, the one where you can't tell who they are – *what* they are. Hey, look –' He was pointing at the previous page. 'You missed this.'

On a page by itself was a photograph of a white

Skye terrier with a moustache, pricked ears and what looked like a tartan bow round its neck. Underneath was written *Angus, January 1930*.

'So it was a dog.'

'Yes,' Julius said, 'it was. And everyone must have known it was. All the people in this album must have known.'

'No,' Jack said, 'not if they weren't family. Ju-ju and the Olive, they only got in because they were friends. They might never have seen the albums. They might not even have seen the photos. They were only little kids. I mean, whose albums are these? Who actually owned them? Who stuck the pictures in?'

Julius for once took time to think, instead of pitching in with an instant theory.

'GG, I suppose.'

'And his children?'

'Richard, Dorothy, Jeremy and John, yes.'

'So Tom and Pat – Auntie Bat – they might not ever have seen them.'

'Go on,' Julius said, his glasses glinting eagerly. 'Go on.'

'If they'd never seen the pictures *in* the albums *with the writing underneath*, they wouldn't have known *what* they were meant to be, would they? Olive and Ju-ju and the Blob. Until you rang up I couldn't make out what they were either. So if someone says, "This is a picture of Robert and Nellie and an alien presence", or, "This is two aliens in a wood", well, they wouldn't know, would they?'

'They might have thought just what I thought,' Julius said. 'Crap photographs.'

'Except this one.' Jack found it and laid it in the middle of the table. 'Alfred, Cecil, Maud, Josephine and unidentified flying object. That isn't a crap photograph, is it? It's as clear as anything.'

The door opened, Steve looked round it. 'Hullo, Jack, good to see you again. Ready to pool information?'

'Pool? Have you got info too?' Julius said. 'Have you been following an independent line of inquiry?'

'Haven't been following a thing,' Steve said. 'Haven't a clue what's going on. Which is why I can't wait to hear what you've come up with.'

J illy had lit the fire in the living room. Shadows dipped and shimmied on the walls and across the ceiling as flames swam up around a long hissing log laid across the fire dogs. She and Steve were sitting in armchairs beside the fireplace, cosy in the half-dark.

Julius looked round briskly. 'We'll need lights. Jack, you move that coffee table on to the rug. I'll get the Anglepoise from the library.'

He went out again. Jack, knowing that it was not only the Anglepoise lamp that he had gone to fetch, looked inquiringly at Jilly.

'Go ahead,' Jilly said. 'Julius rules. Let's have the table over here between us. Can you manage on your own?'

Jack moved the heavy wooden table over to the fire as Julius came in again, gripping the Anglepoise around the throat and with half a dozen of the albums under his arm. He put them on the table, set down the lamp and plugged it in beside the fireplace.

'If it gets too hot we'll have to move back,' he said. 'Don't want to melt the evidence.'

'Aha, the photographs,' Steve said. 'Why did I have the feeling that the photographs would be involved?'

'Because Auntie Bat wanted them so badly,' Julius said. 'And you might as well know,' he went on, 'that if it hadn't been for Jack she'd have got them, very likely.'

'I thought that was my doing,' Jilly said. 'I seem to remember standing in the doorway with a fiery sword crying, "Nothing goes out of this house!"'

'I don't mean the albums,' Julius said. 'What we found she could have taken away and no one would have known a thing about it. Steve, you know when you came into the library on the day of the funeral and caught her yelling at us, well, just as *she'd* burst in Jack had found something. It was a pack of photographs shoved in between the double pages in one of the albums, like that one of you when you were a baby.'

'I'd just got hold of them, just that minute she came in,' Jack said. 'So I pushed them up my sleeve so she wouldn't see them. And then you came in and said that Dad was ready to leave and Auntie Bat was still there, so I hung on to them and didn't say anything.'

'But I saw what happened,' Julius chipped in, 'so that night I rang Jack to find out what it was and he told me it was photos. Now, do you remember how we went through all the albums that evening to try to find out why Auntie Bat wanted them?'

'Vaguely, very vaguely,' Steve said.

'Quite,' Julius said. 'I'm surprised it's even vaguely. But after you two had crashed out I went through them all again and found that sixteen were missing.'

'Only sixteen,' Jilly said. 'Over 150 years I don't think that's too bad. Or too unusual.'

'Ha!' Julius said. 'But it so happens that Jack had *found* sixteen. They weren't lost; they'd been *taken* out. And then we compared notes and realized that we could match every picture to a caption. That's when we knew we had to get the pictures back with the albums to pair them off.'

Jack listened enthralled, as though to a story that he had never heard before. In a sense, he never had heard it before. Julius was letting him star as hero rather than villain, and giving him a share of the credit for Julius's own bright ideas. He suspected that he had had *one* bright idea, but it was too early to be sure.

'Do we get to see these photographs,' Steve said, 'or are they with a forensic lab in Birmingham?'

'No, they're here. Lights!' Julius commanded, and Jilly obediently switched on the Anglepoise lamp. 'Now, never mind where they came from' Julius said, doling them out in a row as if he were playing patience, 'what do you think of these?'

'There's only fifteen,' Jilly said.

'Number sixteen is Something Else,' Julius said. Jack noticed that it was the flying-saucer picture that was missing. 'We'll show you number sixteen when you've looked at the rest.'

Jilly and Steve drew their chairs forward and gazed, like children playing Kim's Game.

'What do you think?'

'I hate to be a downer,' Steve said regretfully, 'but these aren't the kind of pictures I'd put in an album. I'd lose them.'

'Exactly,' Julius said in a kind, forgiving voice. 'So why take them out and keep them? Why not throw them away?'

'Is that a rhetorical question?' Jilly said.

'A what?' Jack was afraid that things were not going as Julius had planned.

'I mean he doesn't want an answer from us because he's got a better one,' Jilly said. No, Julius was in control all right.

'So they're just fifteen pathetic photographs?' Julius said.

'So far.'

'Right.' He took out number sixteen and laid it carefully on the table. 'What about this?'

'Good God,' Steve said. 'It's a flying saucer.'

'Be that as it may,' Julius pronounced, 'it was taken in 1910.'

'A flying saucer in 1910?'

'Look what they're wearing,' Jilly said. 'Definitely pre-World War One. How do you know it's exactly 1910?'

'It's in the album,' Jack said. 'All the dates are written under the pictures. That's why we had to fit them back in. And they do all fit, look.'

Julius had opened the *Sunny Memories* album at the pages where that long-ago picnic party had been caught for ever on film. He took number sixteen and slipped it into the empty space. 'Now look at what it says

95

underneath: *Alfred, Cecil, Maud, Josephine and unidentified flying object, Edgebury Castle, August 1910.*'

'Hm,' Jilly said. 'Edgebury Castle. The mystery voice.'

'Have you ever heard of Edgebury Castle?' Julius said. 'It can't be very far away; somewhere between Goring and Clifton Hampden, we think.'

'No, I haven't,' Steve said. 'But this is extraordinary. Someone took a photo of a flying saucer in 1910 and never said anything about it? Are you sure it isn't faked? It must be.'

'Why?' Julius said. 'If they bothered to fake it, why not do something with it? Why not send it to the papers?'

'Perhaps they did,' Jack said. 'Perhaps that was what happened with Uncle and the aliens.'

'Whose uncle? What aliens?' Jilly said. 'This is getting out of hand.'

'My dad said that whatever the family row was about it had something to do with one of his uncles seeing aliens at the bottom of the garden,' Jack explained. 'But that's all he knows. He doesn't know anything really. Didn't you talk about it after the funeral?'

'We had other things on our minds after the funeral. You haven't shown him these?'

'Haven't shown anyone,' Jack said.

'What about Marty's phone call?'

'Oh, we just asked her if she would look up Edgebury Castle for us, but she couldn't find it either. That's why she rang back – to say that it might be an earthwork. And there's this ditch in one or two of the snaps. It could be a bank or a rampart or something.'

Steve was leafing through the albums. 'They seemed to spend an awful lot of time at Edgebury Castle.'

'That's why we think it must be round here somewhere.'

Jilly had taken the Fresnel lens from Julius and was staring hard at number sixteen. Julius watched her. 'Well?' he said.

'Well what?'

'What do you think?'

'I think,' Jilly said carefully, 'that it *looks* just like a flying saucer: the outer flange . . . the dome . . . and this fuzziness at one side that could be vapour –'

'That's what I thought,' Jack said.

'Would they have had fast enough film in 1910 to be able to take a picture like that?'

'Rather depends on the rate that thing was travelling,' Steve said, 'but in those days it was not so much a question of fast film, it was the shutter speed that mattered. They could take action shots at one-thousandth of a second long before 1910.'

'All right,' Julius said, 'suppose this is a genuine photograph taken in 1910 of a UFO. Why didn't anyone know about it? OK, it was hidden, but it wasn't always hidden. It started off in the album. Why was it taken out with all these others?'

'I'll tell you one thing,' Jilly said, 'they didn't call them UFOs in 1910, and I'll tell you something else . . . whatever they saw coming in from outer space in those days, it wasn't flying saucers.'

'So when was the caption written?'

'I dare say the caption *was* written in 1910,' Jilly said, 'and it means just what it says. Read it carefully: four

97

identified people – Alfred, Cecil, Maud and Josephine – and one *un*identified flying object. Whoever wrote it wasn't to know that one day the skies would be full of unidentified flying objects. Think what it means, what it really means. When people talk about UFOs they've usually got alien spacecraft in mind. But what it literally means is that no one knows what the thing is. An identified flying object could turn out to be a weather balloon or a Frisbee or a Boeing 747. An unidentified flying object is just that – unidentified.'

'Are you trying to tell us something?' Steve said.

'I was,' Jilly said, 'when I was so rudely interrupted. If you really want to know, I think it's somebody's hat.'

'Don't be a spoilsport,' Steve said. 'Just as I was beginning to think that we'd stumbled on something really amazing.'

'Planning a book, are you?' Jilly said, '*Frisbees of the Gods*? No, I'm serious. The outer flange and the dome could just as well be the brim and crown of a hat. And that fuzzy patch we thought was vapour might be a ribbon or a bit of veiling. If you ask me, the person who wrote the caption knew perfectly well what it was – a hat blowing away. They were just joking.'

'Whose hat?' Jack said. 'They've all got their hats on.'

'Just about. The men are clutching theirs, aren't they, and it's windy. Look at those girls' skirts.'

'Why aren't their hats blowing away, then?' Jack asked.

'Hatpins,' Jilly said. 'Six inches of cold steel with a big bead at one end and skewered into your hairdo at the other. Young ladies also found them useful for driving away sex pests.'

'Somebody wasn't wearing a hatpin,' Steve said. 'But if that's a hat it's a woman's hat.'

'Or a child's. A little girl wouldn't have had hatpins.'

'What about the other pictures?' Jack did not want to look at the UFO photograph again. Now that Jilly had said it was a hat, it was hard to believe that they had ever thought it might be anything else.

'I still think they're just very bad pictures,' Steve said. He seemed disappointed too. 'I'd guess someone who didn't like botched shots in their albums took them out but was too sentimental to throw them away.'

'You don't think that someone pretended they were aliens?'

'*Aliens?*'

'Out of the flying saucer.'

'No, I don't. For a start, people didn't see aliens in those days. They used to see fairies, yes. In biblical times they saw angels, wingèd things, fiery wheels, but in the 1920s and 1930s fairies were all the rage. Grown men saw fairies, they wrote books about them. Two young girls claimed to have photographed fairies and people believed them for years. These days it's little green men.'

'No, grey men these days,' Julius said. 'Or grey women. No one seems to know what sex they are.'

'I'm not going to spend the evening sexing aliens,' Jilly said. 'I can smell that the lamb is nearly done. Come through in ten minutes or I shall eat it all myself. And drink all the wine.'

'So what's new?' Julius said, as she went out.

'Sorry, you guys,' Steve said, 'but I don't think the mystery lies here. Or rather there *was* a mystery but we've just solved it.'

'I don't think we've solved anything,' Julius said. 'And why didn't people see flying saucers in 1910?'

'Even though they didn't call them UFOs, people have been seeing strange aerial craft since the 1870s, about the time man-powered flight became a possibility,' Steve said. 'But in those days they were nearly always rocket-shaped, or cigar-shaped. The first flying saucers were seen in 1947 and the term UFO came into use at about the same time.'

'Are you sure about that date?'

'Oh, there's no doubt about it. Some pilot in America reported seeing something and when he was asked about it he said that these craft looked like saucers. It was after that that people began to talk about "flying saucers" and they began to see them. The Roswell Incident was in 1947 too: that was when people claimed that a disc-shaped object had crashed in the New Mexico desert. I'm willing to bet that if Roswell had happened two years earlier – or two weeks earlier – people wouldn't have talked about seeing a disc. And if that pilot had said that his alien craft had resembled giant crocodile clips, that's what everyone else would have seen, and still be seeing. Now, I'm going to open a bottle. What are you two drinking?'

'Juice, probably,' Julius said. 'Don't worry about us, we'll manage.'

He waited until Steve had gone and then swept all the photographs together.

'What are you going to do with them?' Jack asked.

'Jilly's right, isn't she? About the hat. I mean, you can see it's a hat now, can't you?'

'Yes,' Julius said. '*We* can see it's a hat, and I expect that in 1910 they could see it was a hat, because it never occurred to them that it could be anything else. She's right about the caption too, I think. It was a joke, and everybody knew it was a joke.'

'So what's she wrong about?'

'Thinking that this is all there is to it. Look, have you ever seen *Thunderbirds* on television, or any of those old puppet shows – *Captain Scarlet*?'

'Of course I have, often.'

'And they look phoney, don't they?'

'You wonder why people ever thought they were so brilliant.'

'Because,' Julius said, 'when they were first shown they weren't on modern TV sets, were they, with pixels? They were on the old 401 line sets, and even 625 wasn't that much better. Puppets probably looked as real as people, you couldn't see the strings. And the crusty make-up for aliens in SF movies, and monsters in creature features, it looked terrific when they were first shown because no one had ever seen anything like it before. *King Kong* must have looked like the real thing, before *Jurassic Park*.'

'What are you on about?' Jack said, seeing that Julius was definitely on about something.

'Run this past yourself. There's the photograph of Alfred, Cecil, Maud and Josephine and the unidentified flying object, sitting in the album for thirty-seven years –'

'Why thirty-seven?'

'Don't interrupt. You'll see. It sits there for thirty-seven years and everybody knows it's a hat and then one day, in 1947, when people have started seeing flying saucers, somebody looks at it and thinks, "Bloody hell, Auntie Maud saw a flying saucer in 1910."'

'Or,' Jack said, remembering his one bright idea, 'someone who knew what it was showed it to someone who'd never seen it before and said, "Look at this," and the *other* person says, "Bloody hell, Auntie Maud saw a flying saucer in 1910."'

'When did Auntie Maud die?' Julius said, whipping his family tree from between the album pages. 'Shit, haven't got her dates yet.'

'It might not have been Auntie Maud,' Jack said, 'but you know what I mean. And I bet they took it out of the album before they showed it to anyone, otherwise a person who saw it with the rest of the photos would just think it was a hat anyway. If we'd seen it with the others to start with we might have thought that.'

'I think you've got something there,' Julius said. 'I think we both have. So, once X has conned Y into believing that there were flying saucers in 1910, he gets the other manky pictures out and says, "Look, here are the aliens who came down in the flying saucer. And here's the flying saucer, landing in the dark."'

'But you can see that the pictures were taken at different times,' Jack said. 'Nellie and Robert and Angus the Blob were taken in 1929. The clothes are different.'

'Nineteen years,' Julius said. 'It seems like a long while to us because we haven't been alive for nineteen years yet, but it wouldn't seem long to an adult. In the history of the world it's hardly any time at all. Perhaps the aliens kept coming back – that would be the story, wouldn't it? That Edgebury Castle was a site of secret interplanetary power, you know the kind of thing.'

'X knew it was Edgebury Castle. Did Y?'

Julius thought in silence. 'If Y was a friend, or one of the family, they'd know. And if this *is* the beginning of the blood feud, they *would* have been part of the family. You were right! What you said before, if they'd never seen the pictures in the albums, with the captions, they wouldn't know what they really were. But they'd recognize the *place*. They must have known Edgebury Castle like the backs of their hands.'

'What about Wychwood?'

'All you can see is a couple of tree trunks. There were trees at Edgebury Castle – and the flying-saucer landing site.'

'Do you think that's it, then?' Jack said. 'The dread secret, the great blow-up. Somebody blagging somebody else into believing that there *were* aliens at the bottom of the garden?'

'Yes,' Julius said, 'I do, and I'll tell you why. There wouldn't have been any idea of its being a flying saucer before 1947 and there are no photographs after 1948. The pictures stop, don't they? And after that there's just that one other album I told you about, with only us in it.'

'What are we going to do about it?' Jack said.

'Think. Think hard. Meanwhile, we've got two minutes before Jilly starts banging saucepan lids to call us to table. I'll put these albums back. You put the loose snaps in the envelope and take them up to my room. We'll have another look later. Steve and Jilly may think this is the end, I think it's just the beginning.'

Jack shuffled the photographs together and took a last look at number sixteen, at that distant day when Alfred, Cecil, Maud and Josephine had gone out to have their picnic and someone's hat had blown away and they had all run after it –

'Julius!'

'What?'

'Whose hat is it?'

'Come again?'

'They're all wearing their hats, aren't they? Whose hat are they chasing?'

'Could be anyone's.'

'But there's no one else there. They were on their own.'

'No, they weren't,' Julius said, after a moment. 'There was someone else there.'

Out in the kitchen, as he had predicted, Jilly was banging saucepan lids together and Steve was calling, 'Come and get it!'

'Who else was there?'

Julius looked mysterious. 'Come on, Watson, who do you think?'

'An alien?'

'Oh, do me a favour,' Julius said. 'Mind you, I hadn't thought of it either till just now.'

Steve put his head into the room. 'Are you coming through or not?'

'Right behind you, Pater,' Julius said. 'We'll just put the albums away.' As he followed Steve he added,

'Take the loose ones upstairs. Go on, *think*. Who was the other person?'

'I don't know all their names.'

'You don't have to know their names,' Julius said. 'But who took the picture?'

Chapter Eight

Jack would not have minded sharing Julius's room, but he was given one of his own, the third along the landing. Next door to that, he recalled, was the one where Great-Grandad had died. Before he went to bed he put his coat in the cupboard to one side of the empty fireplace. He could have hung it behind the door as he did at home, but he wanted to make sure that the cupboard really was a cupboard and not a way through to the next room, the room that last week someone had died in.

The wall at the back of the cupboard felt reassuringly solid when he tapped it. And he did not believe in ghosts – no, that was not true. He had never yet seen one, but why should he have anything to fear from Great-Grandad, dead or alive?

He switched off the bedside lamp and was pleased to see that Jilly had left the light on in the corridor, for outside the window the sky was darker than he had ever seen it at home. He lay watching the line of light under the door and hoped that no fearsome shadow would suddenly appear in the middle of it. There *was* a ghost, a ghost that had joined them only that evening, just before dinner, that unknown person who had stood behind the camera and taken the photographs at Edgebury Castle. Whoever it was had not appeared in any of the pictures. There were Maud and Josephine, Maud and Alfred, Cecil and Josephine, Cecil all alone, all four together, but never the shadowy fifth who had kept herself out of the frame, always the photographer, never the subject.

Why did he think of that person as 'she'? Because of the hat, the hat that had blown away, a little girl's hat because a little girl would not have had hatpins.

He tried to imagine what she would have looked like, but he had no idea of how little girls looked in 1910. What kind of a camera would she have owned?

Did children have their own cameras in those days?

And where was Edgebury Castle?

By the time they came downstairs next morning Steve had left the house.

'Didn't you say he was at a college?' Jack said. 'Don't they get holidays?'

'The students do,' Julius said, 'but the staff are in and out all through the vacations, and he missed a couple of days last week because of GG and the funeral. He wants to get as much work done as he can now, so that he'll have free time after Christmas when all the stuff in the house has to be packed up and shared out and sold.'

'So that's all the time we've got. If there's anything else to find we haven't got long to find it, especially if Auntie Bat wants those albums.'

'That's going to be the real hassle,' Julius said, 'when they all come back and start demanding things. That's the trouble, nobody's entitled to anything in particular, though if you want to know what I think, Jilly and Steve ought to get something special for enduring all this. But if they did, the All Blacks would say they'd only looked after GG for what they could get. They've more or less said that already. I'd love to keep these albums, because they're fascinating, but if Auntie Bat's got a prior claim – and after all, she's in half of them – I wouldn't stand a chance. No, you're right, we've got to move fast. What do you think we're looking for?'

'Cowgills and Ackroyds,' Jack said. 'What happened to Josephine and Alfred? Who *were* Josephine and Alfred? And who took the picture?'

'Back to the library,' Julius said.

Jilly came into the kitchen. 'I'm off again,' she said. 'Leave the machine on. Listen in if you like and if it's Mystic Marty or anyone else for you two then answer it, when you're sure, but don't even lift the receiver otherwise. Auntie Bat's on the warpath and God knows who else. OK? Steve and I will deal with hostile inquiries this evening. Now, did I hear you mention the library?'

'You did,' Julius said. 'Would I deceive you? You don't mind us ferreting around in there, do you, dear?'

'I do, as it happens,' Jilly said, 'but that won't stop you. What are you looking for now?'

'Anything,' Julius said. 'I promise we'll share what we find. Scout's honour.'

'You in the Scouts? God help us. All right,' Jilly said, 'but be careful. And while you're at it you can list the books as you go.'

'That is not what we had in mind, Mother,' Julius said. 'This is research.'

'The soul of research is method.'

'Are you quoting?'

'No, I made it up, but it's true. If you repeat it often enough I may end up in the *Oxford Dictionary of Quotations*. But I mean it. If you and Jack are looking for clues, look at everything. Don't think that because it doesn't seem interesting it won't be. Just remember to list each book as you check it for the infamous inventory. It'll save me a lot of time. If you have anything in mind it will leap out at you. Of course, you might get a visit from the library angel.'

'What's that when it's washed?'

'Often when you go into the library to look something up, something really obscure, say, some strange impulsion leads you to the right book, makes you open it at the right page – don't look like that, Julius, it often happens. Quite inexplicable.'

'We need a library alien.'

'Oh, aliens. Forget it.'

'Anything in the attic?' Jack said. Surely a house like this had attics.

'I doubt it, and don't even try to get into the cellars. I promise you there's nothing down there. We had a huge clear-out when we first moved in, after Edna died.'

'Didn't Auntie Bat swoop down then?' Julius said.

'Wasn't there a dry run for last week's bombing raid?'

'No, it was a very quiet affair, which is probably why you don't remember much about it, unlike last week's horrorfest. There's nothing up in the attics except old carpets and tea-chests – empty tea-chests. In a house this size we've never needed to keep anything in the attics. You can look, of course.'

Jack was thinking of the loft at home, reached through a trapdoor by a telescopic ladder until Dad had started the conversion. The attic at Stoke Crowell Manor had its own staircase, behind a door at the end of the corridor, next to the entrance to the back stairs. The cupboard under the stairs was empty except for a dustpan and brush, a carpet sweeper and a historic can of Harpic.

The attic, lit by skylights and dormer windows, ran the length of the house, one end divided into tiny rooms – 'Servants' quarters,' Julius said – and the other end an open space with two stone chimneys rising through it. There was nothing to see except sunlight and their own breath in the cold, dry air. The tea-chests and carpets were stacked against the end wall and a lagged water tank stood by the first of the servants' rooms, quietly trickling to itself. They looked into each room in turn but there was nothing at all in any of them, not even cupboards. A row of hooks was screwed into the back of each door for the few clothes that the servants had wanted to hang up. Jack looked out of the windows, hoping to see Wittenham Clumps, but they all faced east, to the trees across the road.

'There's nothing here that Steve and Jilly don't know about,' Julius said.

'What about GG? Couldn't he have come up here on the quiet?'

'By the time we moved in GG wasn't going anywhere,' Julius said. 'He'd already had a stroke. That's partly why Jilly and Steve took over. If he'd gone into a nursing home, the place would have had to be sold to pay for it.'

The tea-chests were as empty as Jilly had said they would be.

'Do you think we should unroll the carpets to see if anything's inside?'

'No,' Julius said. 'Steve did all that when we moved in. They're out of the kitchen and hall and places like that. He wanted to burn them but they're not ours to burn.'

Jack saw an image of the hall carpet, long and narrow, slithering up to the attic like a python, heaving itself from stair to stair. He looked around the empty space – what a terrible waste – and thought of all the centuries of children who might have lived here and played here. For a second, one particular thought struck him, but before he could nail it, examine it, Julius said, 'No, nothing. Let's go back to the library before we freeze,' and he was left clutching at something that disintegrated the more he strained after it, like a dream that broke up as he awoke, leaving him with the certainty that he remembered something but with no idea of what it was.

The library felt almost snug with the heating on.

'Where do we start?' Jack said. 'Top left-hand book-case and work along?'

'No,' Julius said, 'they're just novels and stuff. We'll

start with the big ones at the bottom and work up. They're much older and you find all kinds of things stuck in old books: pressed flowers and holy pictures, letters, cuttings —'

'Secret wills?'

'All I meant was,' Julius said patiently, 'the old ones will be more interesting because even if we don't find anything at least we'll be hopeful. The soul of research is method, but we don't want to die of boredom and despair.' He passed Jack a spiral-bound pad. 'Just record every book as you look at it, author and title.'

'Haven't you ever been through any of these before?' Jack said, as they sat down in front of the lowest row of books and began to tug them out of the shelf. 'This is a dictionary, property of R. J. Aylward.'

'GG,' Julius said. 'Much what you'd expect, it was his house. No, we didn't exactly go through them; there was never any reason to. We were never looking for anything before. We just read them, or looked things up. We must have moved most of them at one time or another.'

'So we probably won't find anything.'

From their point of view it was a desperate waste of precious time, but they could hardly refuse to help Jilly. Still there was a chance that Robert Aylward had left a clue in one of his books, or someone had . . . Jack recalled his sudden thought in the attic, and this time managed to hang on to it. The children who had lived here all those years ago, and played in the attic . . . *which* children? Who had they grown up to be?

'You said this was GG's house. Was it always his?'

'What do you mean?'

'Well, did he buy it or did he inherit it?'

'I don't know,' Julius said slowly. 'I never thought of that. But does it matter?' he asked, after a pause for thought.

'All these Aylwards and Ackroyds and Cowgills – I wondered whose house it used to be. We know who Maud and Cecil were – *you* knew – but what about Alfred and Josephine. Maybe they were the ones who lived here.'

'If any of them lived here.'

'Lived locally, I mean. When they went to Edgebury Castle that day – the flying-saucer day – suppose some of them were visiting the others.'

'We've already thought of that, *you* thought of it, that a lot of the people in the photographs were only visitors and never saw the albums.'

'Yes, but whose albums were they?'

'GG's.'

'Before GG. He wasn't born till 1900. Which family are all the other pictures, the really old ones? They were all Stopfords and Gethins, weren't they? Where did they come from? Where did they go to?'

'OK, abort mission, leave books,' Julius said. 'Back to the albums, you may be on to something.'

They took down the oldest album of all; it was fat, square, fastened with a brass lock. The faces stared out, grim, yellowish, sullen or, like Ewart Rawnsley Stopford Gethin, blurred and mutated. The ones who had risked smiling had had to smile for so long that they looked insane. It did not take long, however, to work out who they all were. The album had begun in

1843 with Arthur Stopford and his wife, Georgiana. One of the Stopford daughters had taken up with a man named Charles Gethin. The next two albums were occupied exclusively by Gethins and the quality of the photographs improved dramatically. In the fourth album Charles's daughter Katherine, Ewart's little sister, married a Joseph Ackroyd.

'New mystery,' Julius said. 'Who were the Ackroyds? Because whoever they were, they turned into us eventually. These albums didn't stay with the Gethins; they came with the Ackroyds. How? What comes next?'

The next album was quite different from the ones before. In the time of the oldest, photography had been an expensive, time-consuming business. You put on your best clothes for it and sat there while the photographer made a long exposure. From 1885 things began to change. Occasionally somebody sat or stood and posed, but the others played tennis, smiled, waved their arms, threw things. The results were not always perfect but there was clearly no question of staying still for a long time.

'What happened?' Jack said. 'What happened so suddenly?'

'Like Steve said, shutter speeds I suppose, and film instead of glass plates and more sensitive emulsions. And the old cameras were huge things on legs. They invented hand-held cameras around this time, snapshots. And then there was the Brownie.'

'Not Elsie-with-the-fairies-type Brownie?'

'George Eastman's Box Brownie camera; came in around 1900,' Julius said. 'Anyone could handle a

Brownie, you didn't have to be a photographer. People developed their own films. One of the Ackroyds must have had a Brownie, perhaps they all did. This next album's wall-to-wall Ackroyds. Look, here's Alfred.'

Alfred was celebrating his ninth birthday. He wore a sailor suit and posed between his two sisters, May, who looked slightly younger, and Elinor, who was a sprawling baby. Within a dozen pages he had grown older, sprouted a moustache, taken to wearing a blazer and boater. He was beginning to look like the young man who would chase the flying saucer at Edgebury Castle.

'But none of these pictures is of Edgebury Castle,' Jack said. 'They hadn't found it yet, I suppose. What about the next one?'

'Method is the soul of research,' Julius said. 'Don't try to get ahead too fast. This looks like the village shop. We're getting closer.'

They reached the end of that album in 1909. Elinor had become a thin little girl with long straight hair. Alfred had gone to Cambridge and graduated, posing in his gown and mortarboard. May vanished in 1905. 'Presumed dead,' Julius said. 'But a lot of people died young in those days. Think of all those Gethin babies who never appeared again. And there are dozens of pictures of gravestones. Look out for Josephine's.' Jack thought he was probably right about May. There were no photographs at all for 1906 and afterwards people were still wearing black, even Elinor.

But things had cheered up again by the beginning of the *Sunny Memories* album.

'The pictures are different too,' Jack said. 'Look, it was always people before – and gravestones – now it's mostly ponies and dogs and kittens.'

'The writing's different too,' Julius pointed out. 'It's very neat, but it looks more as if it's *trying* to be neat.'

Jack flipped ahead a few pages. 'Don't do that,' Julius said, 'method is the soul –'

'I know, I know. But it struck me, it's not just neat, it's getting neater, more grown-up.'

'That's it,' Julius said. 'It's a child. This album belonged to a child. It was a child who took the pictures.'

'Which child? Alfred's grown up, May's died – it must be Elinor.'

'I think it must be, because there aren't any pictures *of* Elinor in this album.'

'So –' Jack turned a page rapidly, but methodically – 'who was she? Who did she turn into? Ah, look. The Aylwards have arrived.'

This picture was captioned *Alfred and Robert Aylward, St Margaret's, 1910*. St Margaret's was a church, the church where GG was buried, not 100 metres away, and the small boy, Robert, was GG, standing with Alfred almost exactly where, eighty-five years later, he was going to be buried.

'Spooky,' Julius said, 'but anyway, GG's finally turned up. Things are becoming clearer. We know that Alfred is Alfred Ackroyd, Robert is Robert Aylward, friend of Alfred. Here's Maud, Robert's big sister, we know that, and here's Josephine and Cecil. The Cowgills are coming, hoorah, hoorah!'

'Is Josephine a Cowgill?'

'Yes, she is, because polite little Elinor has written

Mr and Miss Cowgill underneath. That is Josephine and Cecil, isn't it?'

'Yes, same skirt as the one she wore at Edgebury. They *didn't* have many clothes, did they?'

'Now, we know that Maud married Cecil, we *think* that Josephine married Alfred, or got engaged to him. Josephine is Cecil's sister. So who does that leave for Robert?'

'Robert married Nellie,' Jack said. 'They're in that picture with Angus the Blob.'

'But where *is* Nellie?' Julius said. 'She's not in this album at all. She doesn't turn up till the next one, 1917, in the Red Cross. I'm going to get all this down on the tree.'

He took the family tree out of a wallet file in the drawer, laid it on the table and began to rework it. Jack noticed that the file was full of neatly written notes. There was hardly any need to tell Julius to be methodical, it came naturally. And he knew so much – even without a computer.

Feeling that he should leave the albums until Julius was ready to go on, he went back to the bookshelves. Beside Robert's dictionary was a huge leather-bound volume with the same kind of brass clasp as the first album, and brass hinges as well. It was more like a box than a book and for a moment he let himself hope that it really was a container of some kind, one of those hollowed-out books that hid a revolver or smuggled drugs, but it was a Bible. It had a family tree printed in the front but, disappointingly, no one had ever filled it in.

The next book was almost as large and when he

opened it he found that it was another album; this one contained not photographs but postcards, tidily mounted. There were portraits, flower arrangements, more kittens, cute puppies, actresses, cartoons. A lot of them were landscapes. One of them showed a field with a raised rectangle of grass and a hillock at one end of it. In the distance a cluster of trees broke the horizon. The trees looked familiar. Without saying anything to Julius, he reached for an album and looked up Robert and Nellie and Angus the Blob at Edgebury Castle in 1929. They were the same trees. But the writing at the bottom of the card said nothing about Edgebury Castle. It read *Colman's Camp, nr Blewbury, Berkshire*. Very carefully he eased the card out of its mounting and turned it over. On the back was a franked George V stamp, the postmark dated 23.10.12. On the left-hand side, in sloping blue-black writing, was a note.

Dear Nellie, something to remind you of home. Think of the good times we'll have when you come back for Xmas. Write soon. Mother and Dad send love. Yr Affec. brother, Fred.

On the right-hand side of the card was the address: *Miss Elinor Ackroyd, St Hilda's School, Clacton-on-Sea, Essex.*

Alfred – Fred; Elinor – Nellie. Nellie, the child with the camera who photographed her pony, her kittens, her dogs, her brother Fred and his friends Cecil and Josephine, Cecil's fiancée Maud and her younger brother, Robert. Nellie, a little girl who didn't have hatpins, whose hat had sailed away on a gust of wind just as she pressed the shutter. Nellie was the fifth person at Edgebury Castle and Edgebury Castle was Colman's Camp.

Nellie grew older and was sent to boarding school in Essex. She left school and joined the Red Cross. She married Robert Aylward.

For one instant he had the whole thing in his head. Stoke Crowell Manor had belonged to the Ackroyds; it was home to Fred and May and Nellie. Alfred had died in the First World War, May was dead already. Nellie, the youngest, was the only one left to inherit the house and there she had lived for the rest of her life with Robert and their children: Richard, Dorothy, Jeremy and John. He went on flipping ahead. Alfred had gone, Josephine had gone, Cecil disappeared in 1925 but not before he and Maud had had two children, Tom and Patsy. Tom and Patsy began to grow up in their turn, with Richard and Dorothy, Jeremy and John, their friends Olivia and Juliet, Elsie who was at Wychwood, Angus the dog – one of half a dozen dogs – more ponies, more cats, more friends – and then nothing. Nothing at all after 1948 until Richard married Edna and Steve was born. From 1948 until 1991, when Edna herself died, forty-three years, there were not enough photographs to fill even one album.

What could have happened, what could someone have done, that would make that big happy family split and shiver into so many hostile fragments, so hostile that they scarcely wanted to see each other again and could hardly bear to speak to each other, the thermonuclear family?

Julius was still at work. Jack took out another postcard, this one a seaside picture addressed to Mrs

Ackroyd, Stoke Crowell Manor, Nr Watlington, Oxfordshire; no postcodes in those days, he noted.

3.2.14. Dear Mother, the parcel arrived today. Deevy sweater. Will write tomorrow. Must study Daudet for exam in morning. Ever, your Nellie.

What was a deevy sweater? What was Daudet?

Julius was looking down at him from the table.

'What have you got there?'

'Postcards, Nellie's collection of postcards. Nellie was Elinor Ackroyd, she was the one with the camera. And one of these cards is of Colman's Camp, but it looks like Edgebury Castle to me.'

Julius crash-landed on his knees beside Jack and grabbed at the postcard. 'By George, you've got it! Trouble is, we still don't know where Colman's Camp is, but we were right, it *is* round here, nearer than we thought. Blewbury's not ten miles away, just across the railway. Jilly and Steve might even have heard of it, and if they haven't we can chase it up on a map.'

'But we still don't know what happened, do we?' Jack said. 'We still don't know why those photos were taken out of the albums, and we don't know who took the later ones and we don't know what got done with them in 1948. We're not really all that much further on.'

'Well, we are,' Julius said. 'Remember what we were talking about yesterday, how I thought someone might have pretended that there was something strange about Edgebury Castle. Maybe there really was, really *is*.'

'Why change the name, though?'

'I don't suppose it was actually changed. People just have different names for places, like the earthwork on Wittenham Clumps. I've heard it called Sinodun Camp but it never says that on the map. Local people might have called Edgebury Castle Colman's Camp because someone called Colman lived there.'

As promised, when Jilly and Steve came home they shared their findings.

'I'm impressed,' Steve said, 'although I could have told you my grandmother's maiden name if you'd asked.'

'What's this deevy sweater?' Jack asked Jilly. He guessed it was something that women might know about.

'Deevy – short for divine; early slang for wicked,' Jilly said. 'And Daudet was a French writer. I know, because *I* had to read him at school. As I recall, he lived in a windmill.'

'We've got to find Colman's Camp next,' Julius said. 'Are you sure you've never heard of it?'

'Fairly sure, but we aren't locals and we aren't archaeologists. From that postcard I'd say it was a motte and bailey, or a fortification built round a mound that was already there. Marty was right, an earthwork, maybe Roman or earlier, Iron Age. And I think the reason you never see the mound in the earlier photographs is that it's at the southern end of the fort, so the sun would be behind it and the camera would be pointed the other way. The picture on this card was taken with a bigger camera, without sunlight, and tinted.

'Your best bet is to get an Ordnance Survey map and see what you can find on it. Go into Oxford tomorrow. I'll stand you the fare, and the map.'

Chapter Nine

Before he went up to bed Jack said, 'Can I call home?'

'Any time,' Jilly said. 'You don't have to ask. Give everyone our best wishes, won't you?'

It was Marty who answered the phone. 'Found your castle yet?'

'Almost. You were right, it is an earthwork. It seems to be called Colman's Camp as well.'

'That does sound familiar.'

'You've heard of Colman's Camp?'

'I think so. I can't imagine why, but I'm sure I've read it up somewhere. It has a kind of ring to it. I might even be able to track it down for you. Do you want to call back?'

'I really wanted to talk to Dad,' Jack said.

'I hope you're not suffering too much talking to me.'

'Is Dad there?'

'I'll get him. Look, I'll ring you tomorrow. Here he is. Bye.'

'How are you getting on?' Dad sounded edgy and hopeful at the same time, as if he feared that Jack might have problems to report.

'Ace. Jilly and Steve send their best wishes. Me and Julius are on the track of something.'

'Marty said she thought you might be. No flies on Marty.'

'Right, we think that whatever blew the family up happened in 1948.'

'Ye-e-e-s.' He could hear that Dad did not want to sound too discouraging. 'We more or less suspected that —'

'And we think it's got something to do with some photographs.'

'Incriminating evidence?'

'Dunno yet, Dad. It's not photos of someone committing a murder or anything like that. But you remember that you said one of your uncles saw aliens at the bottom of the garden?'

'That's how the story goes.'

'What actually *happened*?'

'I don't really know much about it. When I was a kid I noticed that everybody at school was loaded down with grannies and uncles and aunties and cousins, but in our family there were just the three of us. You have to remember, families didn't split up nearly so often in those days. But I didn't have anything to do with my grandparents, even; that was really unusual. I asked my father about it but he didn't want to talk, said there'd been a row, and he got angry when I pestered him. And I was old enough to see that he wasn't just annoyed, he was upset, so I let it drop. Then my parents got divorced when I was about your age and he went abroad, I completely lost touch with him. By the time I got around to asking my mother she was very bitter. I don't know how much she knew, but she didn't have a lot to tell me either. She said the whole family was raving mad as far as she could see, but some were madder than others.

'So, of course, I wanted to know more, because I wondered if it was hereditary – you know, passed down from one generation to the next – and if so, would *I* inherit it? I was about fifteen then, just the age to think that being mad might make you rather interesting. But either she didn't know much or she wouldn't say. All I could get out of her was that Tom – who wasn't really my uncle, he was my father's cousin – had got involved with some nonsense about flying saucers, not in America, as you might suppose, but more or less at the bottom of the garden.'

'Tom?' Jack said. 'That's Auntie Bat's brother.'

'Was it? Yes, I suppose it must have been.'

'And it really was at the bottom of the garden?'

'Those were her very words, but I think she was exaggerating, a sour sort of joke. "Everyone else sees flying saucers in the Navajo Desert," she said, "but Tom had to see them at the bottom of the garden." I think she simply meant somewhere near where he lived.'

'Where did he live?'

'Auntie Bat lives near Leeds, but I don't know where they were at the time of the close encounter.'

'Up to 1948 they lived near Stoke Crowell,' Jack said, 'or else they went there a lot. They're in all the

125

photographs, Tom and Patsy, right from when they were babies.'

'You're serious about this, aren't you?' Dad said. 'Real detective work.'

'Yes, and we've found out loads – but we still don't know what happened.' He decided not to mention Nellie's fateful photograph at that particular time. 'Have you heard of a place called Colman's Camp or Edgebury Castle?'

'Since yesterday I have. Marty was talking about it. But remember, I don't know the area at all, except to drive through. Last week was the first time I'd been to Stoke Crowell.'

'Marty thinks she may be able to find out, but thanks anyway. You've been a great help.'

'Why, thank *you*, Son. I never knew you cared,' Dad said. 'Stay in touch. Do we get you back on Thursday?'

'In time for Christmas? Of course.'

'Mum's out. I'll give her your love. See you soon.'

Jack put his head into the living room, said goodnight to Jilly and Steve and went up to tap on Julius's door.

Julius was in bed, studying the contents of his file. He looked up. 'News from home?'

'More info on Uncle and the aliens.'

Julius reached for his notepad. 'Shoot.'

'The uncle was Tom Cowgill, Auntie Bat's brother, and it was a flying saucer he saw, and if it wasn't at the bottom of the garden it was very close to where he lived.'

'And where did he live?'

'They used to live near here, didn't they? When Nellie was taking her photographs the Cowgills were around from May 1910. And Cowgill's an unusual name. There can't be many of them. I've never heard of any before.'

Julius rose from the duvet and shrugged his way into the hairy tweed coat that he used as a dressing gown. 'We'll check with Steve and Jilly before they start snogging.'

Jack followed him downstairs.

'Do they? Still snog?'

'Oh, yes. Once all this hassle's over I wouldn't be surprised if there isn't a new little Aylward to carry on the family name. Jilly's only thirty-six.' He knocked on the living-room door before looking round it.

'Steve, what is the natural habitat of the Cowgills?'

'Come again?' Evidently the snogging had not begun.

'Where do they come from originally?'

'Where they are now. Yorkshire. Auntie Bat's in Harrogate.'

'So what were they doing living round here in 1910?'

'People did move around the country you know, even in those days. I imagine the Ackroyds were from the same neck of the woods with a name like that.'

'Do you *know* where they lived, Cecil and Maud, after they got married?'

'No, I don't, but Cowgills must be pretty thin on the ground round here. It ought not to be hard to find out. Old electoral rolls and so forth. Ask in the County Library tomorrow.'

As they were getting ready to leave the house next morning the telephone rang.

'That'll be Marty,' Jack said. 'Colman's Camp.'

Julius, in the bathroom, called out something, but Jack was already on his way downstairs. As he picked up the receiver Steve's recorded voice butted in, 'Hullo, you've reached the Aylwards, but none of us can get to the phone right now. Please leave your message after the tone.'

He realized that Julius had been reminding him of the answering machine and Jilly's warning about not lifting the receiver until the caller was identified, but it was too late. The tone, a row of bleeps, had sounded and another voice said, 'Jill, Stephen, this is Patricia. I'd be glad if you'd ring me as soon as you get in. I'm sure you'll know why.'

The voice was not friendly and there was no doubt at all that it belonged to Auntie Bat. Of course, she did not know that Jack was on the line as well; he could hold on until she hung up and she would never know. But without stopping to think he said, 'Auntie Pat?'

'So you're in after all, are you?'

'Only me and Julius. Steve and Jilly are out and we're just going.'

'And who are you?'

'I'm Jack Aylward. We met at the funeral.'

The line was echoing unpleasantly which made Auntie Bat sound more unfriendly than ever. Without giving her time to remember *how* they had met, in the library, he plunged on: 'Auntie Pat, I'm glad it's you. There's something I wanted to ask you. Where did you used to live?'

'What on earth has that got to do with you?' Steve

had been right. Jack could hear the Yorkshire in her voice. He did not even pause to invent his lie; it seemed to be ready and waiting for him to say it.

'My sister Marty – you remember, the one with red hair – she's got a friend called Janice Cowgill who comes from ... Aylesbury.' He recalled seeing the word on a map. 'We wondered if she was any relation.'

'Highly unlikely,' Auntie Bat said. '*We* lived in East Hagbourne.' She hung up.

Julius had come into the kitchen and was standing behind him. 'I was warning you about the machine,' he said. 'That wasn't Marty.'

'Auntie Bat. How much did you hear?'

'Something about Marty knowing a Cowgill from Aylesbury. Which I will lay even money was a stinking lie. What are you up to?'

'I was trying to get Auntie Bat to tell me where the Cowgills lived,' Jack said, 'and I did. It was East Hagbourne. Where's that?'

'Somewhere around here, I've heard of it. See if Jilly's taken the road atlas. It'll be under the hall table otherwise.'

The book was lying there with sunglasses, gloves and antifreeze. They opened it on the kitchen table.

'Now, here's us ... Here's Didcot. Where was Colman's Camp near? Blewbury. That's Blewbury. And here's East Hagbourne.'

'It's a sort of Bermuda Triangle,' Jack said.

'Bermuda Quadrangle.'

'No, Stoke Crowell, Blewbury and Didcot, with East Hagbourne in the middle of the short side.'

'The Didcot Triangle. Actually, any three points

form a triangle, unless they're on a straight line,' Julius said.

'Perhaps something odd does go on there, like in the Bermuda one.'

'Oh, *yerse*,' Julius said. 'There was that InterCity train from Cardiff that vanished at Didcot. An entire flock of sheep was teleported –'

'No, I don't mean really happened, just sort of strange rumours. Like you said, any three places make a triangle if you join them up unless they're –'

'On a straight line!' Julius shouted. '*Ley lines.*'

'Rail lines?'

'No, ley lines. Somebody once came up with this theory that there are ancient sites all over the country that can be linked in straight lines. You know, round barrows and earthworks, stones, churches, especially churches dedicated to St Michael – I don't know why. There's even a mark cut in the chalk on the hills near here that's supposed to be on a ley line. Some of them go on for miles, and there's a place in Wiltshire where a whole lot of them meet, a sort of junction: New Age Didcot.'

'That's nothing to do with flying saucers, is it?'

'Oh, yes, it is. Because most of those crop circles I was telling you about are in Wiltshire, and a lot of the cereologists believe that the circles are made by extraterrestrials who are homing in on sites of special power along the ley lines.'

'That's crap.'

'Yes, I know it's crap, but that doesn't stop people believing it. And it *might* turn out to be true,' Julius added cautiously. 'People thought that Galileo's theories were crap once. People used to believe that tomatoes were poisonous.'

'What's tomatoes got to do with it?'

'Well, they aren't poisonous, are they?'

'Did they have New Age in 1948?'

'No, but the ley-line man was years before that. He just got rediscovered in the 1960s with the Age of Aquarius, or something. Oh, I *wish* we had a computer, the Internet –'

'Marty,' Jack said. 'We've got a computer. She'll look up anything we want – but we ought to let her know what's going on.'

'Isn't she going to ring you?'

'Yes, but if we get to her first –'

'No, hang on. We haven't decided what to ask her yet. Wait till we've been to the County Library and looked up ley-line man.'

'Do you think Colman's Camp is on a ley line, then?'

'If it is,' Julius said, 'it might have had a reputation for being a place with strange powers. Uncle Tom might actually have been *looking* for flying saucers.'

'So where does the photograph fit in?' Jack said, 'Nellie's photograph? Do you think he'd seen it?'

'Yes, and he didn't know what it really was. Which means that it wouldn't have been in the album when he saw it, like you said. Otherwise he'd have known that one of those girls was his mother.'

'He'd have known that anyway, wouldn't he? Was Maud still alive in 1948?'

'I don't know. She wouldn't have been all that old, only about sixty, but she might have died in the war, the Second World War. They were all in the Army and the Navy and fire-watching – for incendiary bombs.'

'There weren't any bombs round here, were there?'

'There's a crater over in the woods where that enemy aircraft crashed with its bombs on board.'

'The photo of the trees, all lit up behind?'

'That's the one. And they did fire-watching in Oxford, it's not far away. What was Tom up to during the war? Let's have a look.'

'What about the bus?' Jack said.

'Oh –' Julius waved airily – 'we've missed it. The next one's at 11.40. We'll go for that.'

'Every two hours?'

'We're lucky even to have that,' Julius said.

They went back to the library and looked at the wartime albums. 'Here we go,' Julius said. '1942. Robert – GG – in the Navy, Nellie fire-watching, Patsy, that's Auntie Bat, is nursing, Richard's in the Army – that's my grandfather – John's in the Boy Scouts – he's your grandfather – Jeremy in the Army and Dorothy in the WRNS.'

'We don't know anything about those two, the middle two,' Jack said. 'Jeremy and Dorothy. What happened to them?'

'Jeremy doesn't show up again after 1944. I guess he was killed in action. Dorothy's around in '46 and '47, but only a couple of times in '48. She went to America.'

'And where's Maud?'

'Here,' Julius said, turning back a few pages. 'This headstone: *Maud Cowgill, 1893–1938, dearly loved wife of the above*, which is Cecil, 1925. So she wasn't around to explain the photograph. And nor were Cecil and Alfred and Josephine.'

'But Nellie was,' Jack said.

Julius did not answer. He was flipping backwards and forwards. 'Where's Tom? He was fire-watching too, but he must have done something else. Ah, here he is, in a gown, like Alfred. He must have been at university. I don't suppose they'd have him in the armed forces – look at those glasses.'

'That's sad,' Jack said, holding open one of the pages. The photograph was of a group of people on the lawn behind the manor house: Nellie and Robert standing with Richard and Dorothy; Jeremy and John sat at their feet with Tom and Pat and a dog, not Angus, a spaniel. It was dated 3 September 1939.

'That was the day the war started,' Julius said. 'It was the last time they were photographed all together.'

Beyond the door the telephones began to ring. They both turned at once.

'Get to the machine quick; it only rings twice.'

The ringing stopped as they opened the living-room door, Steve spoke and the bleeps began. Then Marty answered. Julius flung himself at the STOP button and picked up the handset.

'Marty, this is Julius. We're here. Jack, go back to the kitchen, we'll have a three-way.'

'Ready?' Marty was saying patiently, as Jack unhooked the receiver from the wall by the kitchen door. 'OK. I remembered Colman's Camp because of some project we did once about barrows – tumuli, burial mounds, before you start making cracks about wheelbarrows.'

'Madam, you slander us,' Julius said.

'Oh, yeah?' Marty cackled. 'Look, people used to believe that barrows, especially round barrows, were where the fairies lived. They called them Hollow Hills and there were all sorts of legends about people going to some sort of fairy rave for the evening and waking up next morning to find that seven years had passed. These fairies weren't the butterfly sort, they were big tough troublemakers. Now, it wasn't only round barrows; any mound could be a Hollow Hill. There's a motte and bailey at Bishopston, County Durham, that used to be called the Fairy Hill. And . . . Colman's Camp in Berkshire was another.'

'Maybe it was *fairies* at the bottom of the garden,' Jack said.

'Are you going to come clean about Uncle and the aliens?' Marty demanded.

'Briefly, it's this,' Julius said. 'Some time between 1947 and the end of 1948, one of our family, Tom – he wasn't an uncle, but never mind – thought he'd seen a flying saucer somewhere in the vicinity. Jack and I found a photograph of what *looks* like a flying saucer but definitely isn't, taken in 1910 at Edgebury Castle, which seems to be the same place as Colman's Camp. From what you say, there might be some kind of a legend about Colman's Camp. What we'd like to know, Marty, and you might be able to find out for us, is Colman's Camp on a ley line?'

'Oh, my, you are having fun,' Marty said. 'Do you think Uncle Tom's saucer came down the ley line, locked into its potent beam?'

'*We* don't think so,' Julius said, 'but he may have

done. The blood feud was all about Tom and his saucer. We're getting close.'

'So Dad was telling me. But why did everyone *mind* so much? People see UFOs every day. They go on chat shows about it. Serious documentaries are made.'

'They do now,' Julius said. 'Steve calls it Millennium Television: like civilization as we know it is coming to the end of its second thousand years. People think the world will end. Loony prophets arise. But that wasn't happening in 1948, there was still half a century to go. People had only just started seeing UFOs.'

'No, they hadn't,' Marty said. 'They saw things in the nineteenth century too.'

'People have always seen things, but not nearly as often as they do now. UFOs are practically a traffic hazard.'

'Can you find out about the ley lines for us?' Jack asked. 'On the Net?'

'I'll try.'

'Good on you, Coz,' Julius said. They sent each other various permutations of good wishes and hung up.

'I thought of something else just then,' Jack said as they met each other in the corridor, 'only I didn't want to say anything and make life *more* complicated. Let's have another look at the loose photos. Are they in the library?'

'No, in my room, in case they went astray. Why?'

'We've been concentrating on picture sixteen, haven't we, the flying saucer?'

'Yes.'

'And we think we know why it was taken out of the album?'

'Yes.'

'What about the others? The ones with Angus the Blob and the Olive, why were they taken out?'

Julius took the envelope of photographs from his bedside table and laid them out. They stared at them for a few minutes, then Julius said, 'I think you've got the right idea about the aliens. If number sixteen is meant to be a flying saucer, these are what came out of it.'

'Aliens . . . or fairies?'

'That's just it,' Julius said. 'Colman's Camp probably had a reputation for strange sightings. First it was fairies, then it was aliens.'

'But surely all Tom had to do was show Nellie and Robert and say, "Excuse me, is this an alien or is it your dog?"'

'Were Nellie and Robert the kind of people you could say that to? Or would they have rung up the local bin for the men in white coats?'

'Don't forget that Nellie was the one who took the original UFO shot,' Jack said. 'At least, we're fairly sure she was. I don't believe she took any of those other manky ones though. Nellie was good. She knew what she was doing. I think anyone who felt like it stuck snaps in *this* album.'

'Anyone being Richard, Dorothy, Jeremy and John,' Julius said. 'Yes . . . all the writing is different. And maybe Robert – the earlier ones.'

'But not Tom or Pat. They never saw it.'

'So Ju-ju and the Olive is just a rotten picture. One

of them's come out normal and the other one looks like something out of *Communion*.'

'And this one – wasn't it labelled *Elsie and Fairies ha! ha!*?'

'Yes,' Julius said, 'and whoever wrote it must have been thinking of the Cottingly fairies, those two kids Steve told us about who faked the photographs for fun and then found that everybody believed they were genuine and they never had the nerve to confess.'

'These aren't faked, though,' Jack said. 'If they'd been faked they'd never have been put there in the first place. And if they'd been faked I bet they'd be better than this. They were taken out because they were real. But why were they taken out?'

'To show poor old Tom.'

'*Why?* Why pick on poor old Tom? I mean, maybe one of them didn't like him and wanted to make him look a prat, like, "Here, Tom, look. Flying saucer. UFO landing at night. Aliens." And Tom says, "Oh, yes, how interesting." But *why* aliens? Why UFOs?'

Julius said thoughtfully, 'Because he already *had* seen something, that's why. Not in a photograph. He had actually seen it.'

Chapter Ten

To catch the bus they had to cut through the churchyard, walk up the lane and back down to the road. Below them the sun shone on the Oxford Plain. Didcot Power Station and the Wittenham Clumps were veiled in haze and so, beyond them, wherever it might be, was Edgebury Castle, Colman's Camp.

The bus passed through villages and frozen fields, with the Clumps always in view, on the left, up steep hills that were invisible until you came to them, and into Oxford.

'I thought Dorchester was in Dorset,' Jack said. He had seen the name on a signpost and was trying to work out where he was.

'Our Dorchester's the important one,' Julius said, 'or rather it used to be: big Roman settlement and Iron Age before that. The Clumps are just across the river and the earthwork's on top of the one with the most trees. There's another earthwork where the River Thame meets the Thames; the Dyke Hills, it's called. There's ancient remains all over the place. I shouldn't think you could move round here without tripping over a ley line.'

Parts of Oxford looked ancient too, but the centre was modern and crowded and full of the same kinds of shops that they had at home.

'Library first,' Julius said, 'then we'll buy the map.'

'We've got maps in Sittingbourne Library,' Jack said.

'They'll have maps here too, but we need one of our own.'

The County Library was one of the modern concrete buildings. Julius went up to the Archaeological Unit on the second floor and sent Jack to find a book on ley lines. The catalogue listed them under 913.41 in the Dewey Decimal System, which made them seem real and serious. When he found the right section there was only one book, *A Basic Guide to Ley-Hunting*, but the section also included all the books about stone circles, earthworks and ancient monuments. He was working his way through the indexes, looking for a reference to Edgebury Castle or Colman's Camp, when Julius came to find him.

'Wizzo!' he said, when he saw the *Basic Guide*. 'But is that the only one?'

'Looks like it. Or the rest must be out on loan – all those ley lines crawling with ley-hunters. Any luck upstairs?'

'Sort of. All that side of the river used to be in

Berkshire before they moved the county boundaries in 1974, so they haven't got much material here.'

'The postcard said Blewbury, Berkshire, didn't it?'

'So it did. Anyway, I looked up Edgebury and Colman's Camp in the card index, but there's nothing there. I *could* make an appointment with the archaeologist, but she's not here today and by the way the librarian looked at me I think we'd better get Jilly or Steve to do it. Don't I look respectable?' he demanded plaintively, in his ankle-length black coat and the mirror shades. Jack could see the librarian's point.

'There's an Ordnance Survey map here,' Jack said, 'let's have a quick look. Edgebury might still be in Berkshire.'

'They won't have it upstairs, then. But look at all this; there's a fort marked at Aston Upthorpe, right next to Blewbury. And what's this – Lowbury Hill, a tumulus. Here's the Ridgeway, one of the oldest tracks in Britain.'

'Is it a ley?'

'Leys are straight. The Ridgeway's all over the place, look. It goes along the ridge of the Berkshire Downs. Ridge-way, geddit?'

'Why isn't Edgebury on here, or Colman's Camp? I mean, we *know* it's a real place.'

'Too small for this scale, I expect,' Julius said. 'Put it away. We'll take the *Basic Guide* and go for a map at Blackwell's.'

The bookshop specialized in maps. While Julius was locating sheet 174, Jack looked along the shelves. On one was a row of maps folded into cream and brown slip covers. On the fronts it said, *Reprint of the original*

Ordnance Survey. Sheet 71 was the Oxford and Reading area. He grabbed it and took it over to Julius. 'Let's get this too.'

'I didn't know about these,' Julius said. 'We'll have them both. We must be able to find *something*.'

The shop was too crowded to unfold the maps and time was running out for the bus.

'We'll cut through the Bodleian,' Julius said as they left the shop. He crossed the road and led the way up steps, under arches and through courtyards among great silent stone buildings, dodging groups of tourists with guidebooks and cameras.

'Of course,' he said, 'this is where we ought to be.'

'Why?'

'This is the Bodleian. It has a copy of every book ever published in this country, nearly.'

'Can't we go in?'

'No, it's the University Library. You have to have a special Reader's Ticket. But Steve's got one,' Julius said. 'He can't take books out but we could send him in to find what we want. When we know what we want.'

At home they cleared the bedroom floor and opened out the two maps they had bought, alongside the older one from downstairs. The twentieth-century maps were in colour, the original facsimile in black and white, and at first it looked more crowded than the others, in spite of there being so few towns and built-up areas.

'It's the hills,' Julius said. 'They didn't use contour lines so they marked the hills with shading.'

Jack had not known quite how hilly the area was.

The markings were so thick and dark it was almost impossible to read the lettering in places.

'Even the lens doesn't help much,' Julius said. 'Let's take this slowly. The newest map is 1993, G G's is 1919 and the first one is 1830. We'll compare notes, starting with 1993. Here's Aston Upthorpe and Aston Tirrold. Here's Lowbury, next to Unhill Wood, and they're all on the 1919 map as well. What have you got on yon historic fax?'

'It says Unwell Wood here,' Jack said, straining his eyes over the old map. 'And Aston Tirrold is Aston Tirrel. Names *do* change. Blewbury's spelt Blewberry, like it grows on a bush.'

'I've got a fort marked on Blewburton Hill at Aston Upthorpe in 1993,' Julius said. 'Now, in 1919 it says *Danish Camp*. What have you got for 1830?'

'There's a sort of shaded ring on Blewburton Hill, but it isn't named,' Jack said. 'There's all sorts of markings like that. The one on Wittenham Clumps is the same – a ring but no name. On Sinodun Hill.'

'That's Castle Hill now,' Julius said, 'and it's marked as a fort. In 1919 it was Castle Hill and it says *Camp*. I wonder if places only got named on maps if they'd actually been excavated. If people thought there were fairies living in the Hollow Hills, they wouldn't be down as mottes or tumuli, would they?'

Jack leaned across to look at the middle map, 1919. 'Didn't you mention Segsbury once? There's a place here on the Ridgeway that says *Letcombe Castle or Segsbury Camp*. On the old map it says – I can't hardly read it – it just says *Letcombe Castle*.'

'Doesn't even say that on the new one,' Julius said.

'It's marked *Fort*, like Sinodun. So once upon a time they were called camps *or* castles, and now they're called forts.' He stared glumly at the three maps. 'South of Blewbury it's a built-up area for earthworks. Edgebury could be anywhere.'

Jack found that he was grasping at another of those slippery, evasive thoughts. 'Just a minute,' he said. 'Remember the Didcot Triangle – what gave you the idea about ley lines? Didcot, East Hagbourne and Blewbury *are* in a straight line. If we just keep following it . . .'

'It's worth a try. It's probably what Tom had in mind anyway. Time to consult the *Basic Guide*,' Julius said. 'Here we are. Alfred Watkins – that was his name! – Alfred Watkins rediscovered ley lines in the 1920s. Orthodox archaeologists don't believe in them but nevertheless alignments do exist. Right, now, ways of spotting a ley: they must have been laid down by surveyors or they wouldn't be straight . . . Possibly the Long Man of Wilmington – that's a hill figure in Sussex – is a surveyor because he's carrying two poles *and* he's on a ley line . . . Listen to this! Many of the ley sightings would have been fixed by means of beacons. Places with Cole or Cold in their names may refer to Colman the surveyor, from *coel*, Welsh, meaning light. Colman's Camp. It must be on a ley. Get a ruler.'

'Which bit of each place do we use as a marker?' Jack said.

'The churches, to start with. Does that work?'

'There's two churches in Didcot.'

'Use the one that lines up with East Hagbourne and Blewbury, then. Yes?'

'Yes.'

'*Three places in alignment are not enough to prove the existence of a ley*,' Julius said, reading from the book. 'Well, three's what we've got. Is there anything else?'

'There's a tumulus just south of Lowbury Hill – but the line doesn't go through it.'

Julius read, '*Leys often run along the sides of mounds, like tangents, not through them.* Does that help?'

'Yes . . . the line just touches it – and there's another fort here, further along, on the other side of the line.'

'Hold the ruler steady.' Julius drew a pencil along it. 'Now we've fixed it. Find Lowbury on GG's map. What does it say?'

'Lowbury Hill – *Roman Camp and Tumulus.* And that other fort, just below it, that says *Roman Camp* too.' Jack took the ruler and laid it on the oldest map.

'Is it there? I can't see with your fat head in the way.' Julius craned his neck but did not push.

'Lowbury Hill, nothing else marked,' Jack said. 'But there's another of those rings where the fort is. It's got writing . . . something Hill . . . Edge . . . Edgebury Hill.'

'Are you sure?'

'See for yourself. It must be the right place; but it doesn't look like a Roman camp on the postcard.'

'The Normans often built on Roman remains, and the Romans probably built on Iron Age earthworks. Stands to reason, if you'd got a good defensive site you wouldn't waste it, would you? Stamp your little foot and say, "I *won't* put my fortress here. Those nasty rough Britons got here first and *spoiled* it."'

'Well, no,' Jack said, 'but I wish they'd sort their names out.'

'Never mind,' Julius said, 'we've got four, possibly five places in alignment. Even if Didcot isn't one of them, we've still found a line reaching from Edgebury Castle right to Uncle Tom's doorstep.'

'Or the bottom of his garden.'

'It says here,' Julius read, 'that in 1954 there was an outbreak of UFO sightings in France, and a researcher called Aimé Michel charted alignments of landings – *landings?* – and low-level sightings and called them orthotenies. In the early 1960s a British UFOlogist and ley-hunter said that orthotenies and ley lines might be the same thing.'

'It wasn't Tom, was it?'

'No, Tony Wedd. Anyway, the 1960s are much too late. Whatever Tom saw was more than ten years earlier. But he might have had the same idea.'

'Especially if he'd had a close encounter – or thought he had.'

Jilly was calling from the foot of the stairs. Julius went out to answer.

'Have you checked the machine since you got in?'

'No – but we accidentally intercepted a call from Auntie Bat before we went out. Sorry.'

'I know,' Jilly said, 'I've been listening to it. Anyway, there's a message for Jack, from his mother. Would he ring home and tell her which train he'll be catching tomorrow? And Marty has something to tell him.'

Julius came back into the room. 'You hear that? Going tomorrow?'

'Mum said home by Friday. It's because of Christmas.'

'Oh, dear me,' Julius said, 'and I did hope we'd crack it before you went.'

'I can come here again afterwards,' Jack said, 'as soon as it's decent. Or you could come down to us.'

'Yes, thanks. I will, some time. But I think what we're looking for is going to be here, don't you? On that ley line?'

Jack left next morning with a list of things to think about. Jilly drove him to Didcot and Julius came up on to the platform to see him off.

'Well, Happy Christmas and all that,' Julius said.

'What about you? Are you getting a tree or decorations? It's only four days to go.'

'We always do everything at the last minute. I expect we'll pick up a tree on the way home, or we can saw a bit off something in the garden. I'll spend the evening cutting snow crystals out of old newspapers and we'll spray fake frost on the windows.'

'Sounds terrific.'

'Don't worry about us. We'll have a huge fire, and food and drink and carols on CD This is the first chance we've had for years to let rip. We aren't used to it. Couldn't let rip with poor old GG upstairs. I see your train coming, down there by the cooling towers. Ring the minute you get back and discover what Marty's found in cyberspace.'

Jack sat on the train, by the window, and watched Julius's waving figure grow smaller. Then he looked out across the frosted fields to the Wittenham Clumps. When they vanished, he shifted to the other side of the carriage and gazed westward, towards Blewbury, Lowbury, Edgebury, wondering what was there and if they would ever find it.

After a while he took out the wad of notes that he and Julius had compiled and duplicated, but they seemed to make little sense without the maps, the photographs, the feeling that all the answers must lie close around them. Even the new, improved family tree looked bogus. The further he travelled from Stoke Crowell, the stranger it all seemed. He had spent three days without a computer, without watching videos, without playing football; without any of the things he had thought he could never live without. He was glad to be going home for Christmas, of course he was, but he could hardly wait for it to be over so that he could be with Julius again in the thick of the quest.

But by the time he got to Paddington it all seemed like something that had happened years ago, nothing to do with him, which was, in a way, exactly the case.

At Sittingbourne Station Marty was in the booking-hall.

'Thought you'd gone for good,' Marty said. She passed him a sheet of paper. 'For your eyes only.'

'What's this?'

'Print-out. All I could find out about ley lines on the Internet. Trouble is, it all seems to be American.'

'Do Americans have ley lines?'

'They seem to think so, especially on the West Coast. Anyway, it's not much, but it's better than a poke in the eye with a sharp stick. I hate to say this, but I think you're better off using a library.'

Mum was waiting in the car.

'I take it you had a good time.'

'Yes. Yes, I did. Can I go back after Christmas?'

'Funny you should say that. Jilly rang up as soon as she got home from taking you to the station and invited us all over for New Year. She says it's a shame to waste all that space while they've got it.'

'Did you say yes?' He wondered if he wanted the whole family at Stoke Crowell with him. But he and Julius could stay out of the way of everyone else. And two cars; they could get lifts.

'I'll have to check with Dad but I should think he'd be delighted, so I've said yes, please, provisionally.'

He put Marty's print-out in his pocket to read later and as soon as they reached home he raced upstairs with it, scarcely pausing to look in at the decorated tree in the living room. His room was in the same state as he had left it. The only difference was that Mum had put a clean sheet, duvet cover and pillowslip on the bed, as she did every Thursday, so that he could change the linen first thing in the morning. He sat down and read the print-out.

This was something way beyond the matter-of-fact information in the *Basic Guide to Ley-Hunting*. Ley lines, he learned, are cosmic forces originating from outside of planet earth. They penetrate and leave the earth vertically at nodes, going down 265 feet, then making a right-angled turn and continuing in a perfectly straight line. The cosmic force gets out again by making another right-angled turn, travelling straight through the earth and exiting on the other side. A person who stands on a ley line tends to be hyperactive. Various people have reported that when on a ley line they experienced 'energizing white fuzziness', 'faint smooth energy' and a 'glowing lane of light that went with the flow'.

He went downstairs, telephoned Julius and read Marty's findings.

'American ley lines must be different,' Julius said. 'Like flakier. I mean, with all the ley lines there are around here you'd think the joint would be jumping, but people seem fairly normal. The Thames Valley is not noted for hyperactivity, nor groves of sacred cosmic light. But is that all? I thought the collected wisdom of the entire history of the world was supposed to be out there in cyberspace.'

'It's only there if somebody puts it there,' Jack said. 'Marty thinks we'd be better off in a library.'

'I agree,' Julius said. 'On the other hand, all this about cosmic forces and fuzzy white energy sounds more like Uncle Tom than you and me crawling about with maps and rulers. In the ley-hunting book there's a lot about the Straight Track Postal Portfolio Club. They used to keep in touch with each other about leys that they had spotted.'

'Is it still going?'

'It closed in 1948. Is that significant, do you think?'

'I wonder if Tom belonged to it.'

'I see Tom as a lone operator. We're going shopping in Oxford tomorrow. I'll snout around and see if I can find anything else. I believe we'll be meeting again shortly.'

'New Year. This time next week. Happy Christmas.'

'And the condiments of the see-saw to you and yours,' Julius said.

He had never thought that Christmas could be an anticlimax. It was something you felt nostalgic about as soon as it was over, started to think about again almost immediately, looked forward to all year. The whole autumn term was lit up by the thought of it glowing at the year's end.

This year it would count for hardly more than a pleasant interruption to more pressing business. Like Julius, he had better go shopping tomorrow; he had not even bought any presents yet. He went back upstairs and stood in the middle of the bedroom. Something was bothering him. For some reason, when he came home he had been relieved that Mum had not changed the bedding in his absence. Why?

He called over the banisters, 'Do you want me to put the bedclothes in the laundry basket?'

'No, don't bother. You've hardly slept here since the last change. I put the clean stuff there out of force of habit – just put it back in the airing cupboard.'

Then he remembered. Somewhere in the room, under the bed or in it, possibly, was the original wrapping from the photographs that Julius had thought might be important. He went back and pulled the duvet off the bed; nothing there. He looked underneath and found a pen that he had lost weeks ago. Then he leaned over and ran his hand along between the bed and the wall. Something was there, something that almost crackled but was slightly too soft. He pulled it out. It was a sheet of white paper, still folded along the lines where it had encased the photographs. It was printed on one side only, with a design like a banknote, only it was far larger than any banknote he had ever seen, but it said £5 plainly enough. And there was something scrawled on the reverse in furious scratchy letters: *You can have this back too, you swine. I never want to speak to you again.*

He sat on the bed and stared at the spiky, spiteful letters. *You swine.* Nobody called anyone a swine, these days; there were much worse things to call them, but even so that distant anger shook him over the years, the anger and, yes, the hurt, that raged out of those sixteen words. *I never want to speak to you again.* Someone had betrayed whoever wrote them, he was sure of it. *You can have this back too.* Have what back . . . the wrapping paper? Could it be a real five-pound note? Printed in black on white, on one side only, it looked like a half-finished forgery. *Too.* As well as what? The photographs. Someone had lent the photographs to somebody else who had – done what with them? Who was it? Tom? Or had Tom written the message?

His first thought was to go down and show the enormous fiver to Mum and Dad, but that would be unfair to Julius. However interested Dad might be, and he *would* be interested, Julius must know about it first.

It was only later, while he was getting ready for bed, that he noticed a song had been going round in his head all evening.

> *The Owl and the Pussy-cat went to sea*
> *In a beautiful pea-green boat.*
> *They took some honey, and plenty of money,*
> *Wrapped up in a five-pound note.*

It was years since he had heard that song. It must have been on a kiddy tape in the car. He had not even realized that he knew the words, but he remembered hearing it over and over again and always supposing that it was a joke. Well, it was, the whole song was a joke, but he had never imagined that you really could wrap anything in a five-pound note. In the modern ones you couldn't, but this thing here, it was about the size of a sheet of A5.

Back downstairs he went, to the living room, where Marty and Mum were watching *High Plains Drifter* for the millionth time and had just reached the part where Clint Eastwood makes the citizens paint the town red. They looked round irritably when he came in.

'Where's Dad?'

'Down the club,' Marty said, switching the video to PAUSE. A furious stubbly face hung on the screen, snarling.

'Mum, do you know how big five-pound notes used to be?'

'What? I can just remember them being bigger than they are now, but they were worth something in those days. They had to be bigger than pound notes.'

'Pound *notes*?'

'Yes, in the Dark Ages we had pound notes and ten-shilling notes – fifty pence. I remember when the fifty-pence coin came in people used to call them "squares". A pound was worth something then too.'

High Plains Drifter was forgotten, he could see. Fond memories were in the air.

'Can you remember when they were really huge?' He gestured with his hands.

'That's a tea-towel you're describing. No, *I* can't remember, but they used to be much larger than any other note. And they were white – I've seen pictures. What's all this about? Julius, I suppose.'

'Sort of. Can I ring him?'

He went to the kitchen extension and dialled.

'I thought it would be you,' Julius said. 'Guess what I'm doing. I've hijacked all the postcards out of the album and I'm reading through them. I think Tom and Dorothy were in love, or Tom was in love with Dorothy. He sent her the sloppiest pictures. What have you got to report?'

'One, we're definitely coming for New Year –'

'I know. Your father rang Steve.'

'But I can come back earlier if you like.'

'I know that too. I do like. What's the next thing?'

'You remember that when I found the photographs they were wrapped in paper and you thought it might be important.'

'Yes.'

'You may be right. I've found it. It's a five-pound note, one of the old kind. Huge.'

'Very weird. Is that all?'

'No, someone wrote on it, *You can have this back too, you swine. I never want to speak to you again.*'

'Ah,' Julius said. 'Now we *are* on to something.'

'Christmas wasn't too dull I hope?' Dad said, dropping him at the station on Wednesday morning.

'No, it was *wicked*, you know it was. It's just –'

'That you and Julius have got something better to do? Are the rest of us ever going to find out what you're on to?'

'When the rest of you come over on Sunday we'll tell everything,' Jack said, 'if we know everything by then.'

'You can't tell me anything now?'

Jack hesitated. Dad was not simply being curious or taking a fatherly interest; he wanted to know what was going on, urgently wanted to know it.

He said, 'If I show you something, will you keep it a secret, not tell Mum or Marty?'

'Careless talk costs lives?'

'We don't want to – well, it's not their family, is it?'

'I hope you don't mean what I think you mean.'

'Marty being adopted? No.'

'It's her family as much as yours.'

'It's not really mine either,' Jack said. 'Well, it is, but only just. Two weeks ago it hardly wasn't. It was you, I meant, your family. So I'll show you what we found – we found a lot of things, but I've only just realized what this is.'

The car had pulled up in the station forecourt. Jack unzipped the travelling bag that lay between his feet, took out the Uncle Tom data and extracted the five-pound note.

'Good God, where did that come from?' Dad said, holding it open on his lap.

'We found it wrapped round some photographs – and we'll show you those too. Julius has got them.'

'It's even got the date printed on it, 11 June 1945. I've never seen one this old.' Dad was turning the note over, expecting to see a design on the back. Then he noticed the words written on it and Jack felt his shock.

'Dad, what's the matter?' It was like Billy Bones getting the Black Spot in *Treasure Island*. 'Dad. Do you know what it means?'

'No,' Dad said, 'I don't know what it means, but I can tell you who wrote it. That's my father's handwriting.'

They sat for a few minutes without speaking. At last Dad said, 'Well, I won't grill you, and there's only five minutes before the train arrives and you've promised to reveal all at the right moment, so I'll wait. But that was a shock, Jack. It's nearly thirty years since I've seen that writing. Who was it sent to?'

'We don't know. Are you *sure* it's his?'

'Oh, you're a real sleuth, aren't you?' Dad said. 'Never let sentiment get in the way of facts. Yes, I am sure. It's very square, isn't it, and those funny Greek Es, like a V on its side with a line through it. Well, I can't imagine what you're sniffing out, but this looks as if it might be part of it. A blast from the past. "Swine" was about the worst thing you could call someone in those days – in polite society.'

Jack was already on the train when a thought came to him, something which had not struck him or Julius before. 'Dad, is Tom still alive?'

'I don't think so,' Dad said. 'Auntie Bat would know, of course. I'm sure there was no one called Tom at the funeral. She was on her own, wasn't she?'

'How would we find out? Without asking Auntie Bat?' The train was moving.

'I'll think about it. See you on Sunday. Cheers!'

Jack wondered why they had been so clueless. If

Auntie Bat was still rampaging around, why wasn't Tom? And he wasn't.

Because he was dead?

When did he die?

His last appearance in the albums was in 1942, but clearly this was not when he saw – whatever he did see. What was he doing during the war?

Chapter Eleven

'This was written by John,' Jack said, when they had settled in the library. He produced the five-pound note and passed it to Julius. 'At least, Dad's sure it was. John was his father.'

'Soon check,' Julius said, pointing to the table. The photograph albums had been cleared away. In their place Julius had laid out the postcards, face down, so that the writing showed.

'What order are they in?'

'Just as they came out of the album, chronological. They must have been put in as they arrived. Nellie's mother started it, but it was finished off by Dorothy; nearly all the later ones are written to her, although she's put some others in, because she liked the pictures, I suppose. This one's from John, and this. It's the same writing. And this very last one, that's his as well.'

11th December 1948. Dear Dot, hope you have a good crossing. Strange not to see your ugly mug at breakfast any more. All the best, Sis. Love, John.

'She was the one who went out to America, wasn't she?' Jack said. 'He must have sent that just before she left.'

'Why didn't she take it with her, then? Why did she leave the album here?'

'Perhaps she meant to come back for it and never did,' Jack said. 'Perhaps something happened.'

'We know something happened. This just pinpoints the date again, 1948. Something else is about to happen, actually, only I didn't want to set Jilly off in the car. Auntie Bat's coming tomorrow.'

'Why?'

'She says she's been in touch with everyone – those she's speaking to, anyway – to find out what GG promised them and she's going to "assist" Jilly to sort it out before the rest of the stuff goes for sale. If there's anything left to sell by the time she's finished. Steve says she'll need a moving van to shift the loot. And I bet she's still got her eye on those albums.'

'Can't they stop her taking them?'

'Not very well. They wouldn't fetch much if they went on sale and it would be suspicious if Jilly and Steve said no, especially if no one else really wants them.'

'We really want them.'

'Yes, but I don't think she'd be very pleased if she knew why.'

'What about the loose ones and the five-pound note?'

'We'll cross that bridge when we come to it,' Julius said. 'Sufficient unto the day is the evil thereof. Or, to put it plainly, let's wait and see. Anyway, back to the fiver. Does your dad know where it came from?'

'No, and he didn't ask. But he's dying to find out. Look, for some reason John had those photographs. We don't know if he took them out of the albums himself, but at some point he had them in his possession.'

'I think,' Julius said, 'I think he must have got them for someone else, someone who paid him five pounds to do it.'

'Five pounds isn't much.'

'It was then. It was a hell of a lot. And he wasn't very old, was he, John? Only about eighteen.'

'And he was sorry he'd accepted it and sent it back, do you think?'

'Yes, definitely. But he was sending back the photos too. Sending them here, to this address, or to someone who came here afterwards. Where was *he*?'

Jack looked at the last of the postcards, sent to Miss Dorothy Aylward, The Manor House, Stoke Crowell, Oxon. It was postmarked Harrogate. 'He was staying with the Cowgills,' he said. 'Look, here's another. Harrogate. Steve said Auntie Bat lived in Harrogate.'

'This one isn't from him, though,' Julius said. 'It was posted in York but someone's written *10.3.48 Harrogate* on it. This is Tom's writing. *Dear Richard* – that's my grandfather – *many thanks for the information. Any pictures of our Camp will be welcome. V. grateful for your kind interest. T.*'

'Our Camp – Colman's Camp. He was *asking* for pictures. Are there any more from him?'

'There's some deeply slushy ones to Dorothy, but they're much earlier. Wait a bit, here's one from June 1947. *Dear Aunt Nellie, thanks for your charming note. I'll put a copy in the post at once. With kindest regards, Tom Cowgill.*'

'Copy?' Jack said. 'Copy of what?'

'A book,' Julius said positively. 'He'd had a book published and Nellie had written to congratulate him and he wrote back and said, Thanks very much, I'll send you one.'

Jack looked up at the shelves. 'Then maybe it's still here.'

Julius leaped up. 'You start bottom right, I'll start top left. We'll meet in the middle if we don't find it first.'

It was a very slim volume when Julius discovered it, almost hidden between two fat novels. He levered it out and they looked at it, the size of a paperback with dark-yellow cloth boards and gold lettering on the spine: *The Straight Way from Oxenford* by Thomas Cowgill. When they opened it a slip of paper fell out, a cutting from a newspaper review.

Mr Cowgill has lived in North Berkshire for much of his life and has devoted much time to the investigation of ley lines in the Thames Valley. Enthusiasts will welcome this little book as a vindication of their beliefs in "The Old Straight Track" (see Alfred Watkins, 1925). Mr Cowgill is currently preparing a second volume on a similar theme.

They looked through *The Straight Way from Oxenford*, 'Which is the old name for Oxford,' Julius said. It seemed to cover much of the same ground as the *Basic Guide to Ley-Hunting*, but without photographs. Instead it was illustrated by neat, pale pencil drawings of churches, barrows and earthworks, and diagrams of ley alignments, all signed 'T. Cowgill, 1946'. On the title-page was written, *To dear Aunt Nellie with fondest love, Tom*, but the dedication read, *To the Memory of my Mother and Father and Aunt Josephine.*

'"To the Memory of": that's Josephine out of the way, then,' Julius said ruthlessly.

'Is our ley in there?' Jack said.

Julius turned to the index. 'Doesn't look like it – oh, yes, page 25. It's a footnote. Earthworks, e.g. Colman's Camp, Berkshire. This is mainly about leys crossing in the middle of Oxford and trying to link them with other sites. Our ley misses Oxford altogether and none of the leys in here goes anywhere near Colman's Camp. Still, this is more proof that it was important to him. I think he must have been saving it for the other book.'

'What other book?'

'It says he was preparing a second volume on a similar theme. And he wrote to Richard saying that pictures would be very welcome. Pictures!'

'The photographs?'

'The photographs. Where was that card he sent Richard? Look, the address: Richard wasn't here, he was in Berlin.'

'After the war.'

'It was occupied by the Allies; he must have been

posted there. So he got his little brother John to pick out the photos.'

'What, told him to get all the really peculiar ones –'

'They were probably a family joke, like the UFO one. John would have known what he wanted,' Julius said. 'So John got the photographs out of the albums and sent them to Tom. And if you ask me, he didn't know what was going on, John didn't. In fact, he probably sent them to Richard without knowing why Richard wanted them. Richard sent them to Tom.'

'And Tom put the photos in a book.'

'He put them in a book and then the others turned round and said, "Yah, boo, we were only fooling, there aren't any flying saucers at Edgebury Castle."'

'Why would he think there were?'

'He'd seen *something*, remember. And Dorothy married an American – he may have been the one who first mentioned flying saucers to her. Anyway, the family set Tom up and he fell for it.'

'We'll have to find the other book.'

They searched the shelves, taking out every volume and examining it, and then, when that proved fruitless, taking them out again and looking at the backs of the shelves, but after three hours there was no doubt: Tom Cowgill's second book was not there.

'He might never have finished it,' Jack said. 'That bit in the paper only said he was preparing it.'

'You know, I almost hope he didn't finish it,' Julius said. 'Just imagine how he would have felt, all his theories and proof, and then it turns out to have been a hoax, and his family and the girl he loved were all in it together.'

'We don't know about Dorothy,' Jack said, 'but this must have been what caused the great bust-up. Tom and Pat didn't want anything else to do with the Aylwards and John was furious because he thought he'd been *used*.'

'Which he had, if we're right. Say, Dorothy is in America – for the first time – Richard's in Berlin, GG's in the Navy, Jeremy's dead, John's only just left school, I should think. He was the only one still at home, him and his mother, Elinor – Nellie.'

'I wonder if she was in on it too.'

'I wonder *why* they did it. It's a sort of bullying, isn't it, all of them ganging up on Tom like that. And John didn't realize what was going on at first, I suppose. He just got the pictures he was told to get and passed them on to Tom – no, to Richard. He must have been *with* Tom when Tom found out what had happened, and he got all the pictures together, wrapped them up in a fiver and sent them back to – who did he send them back to?'

'It must have been Dorothy or Richard. No, not Dorothy. That card he sent her before she sailed was friendly, wasn't it, and he couldn't have sent them to America or they wouldn't be here.'

'To Nellie?'

'It was Richard, definitely. He wouldn't call his mother a swine, would he?' Jack said. 'I shouldn't think he'd say it to his sister either.'

'No, he'd probably call her a cow. "You swine" sounds sort of man to man, doesn't it?'

'Or pig to pig.'

*

Auntie Bat rang that evening to announce that she had arrived in Oxford and would be joining them first thing in the morning. Jilly immediately felt a headache coming on.

'It's the cosmic forces at work,' Julius said. 'Auntie Bat is coming down the ley line to get you. Do you feel waves of energizing white fuzziness?'

'Yes,' Jilly said. 'It's called a migraine.'

'Actually,' Julius said to Jack later, 'I don't feel nearly so ready to hate Auntie Bat as I used to. It's crazy, whatever our ancestors did to her brother, to take it out on us and Jilly and Steve, but in a way you can sort of see why. She may only have come to the funeral to see if she could get her hands on those photographs.'

'Or the second book,' Jack said. 'Or perhaps she just wanted to make sure that GG was really dead, like dance on his grave.'

'Come to think of it,' Julius said, 'where *is* GG in all of this? What did *he* do?'

'Nothing, maybe. If he was in the Navy, he might have missed the whole thing.'

'We'll have to speak to her tomorrow,' Julius said. 'We can't ask her right out, she'd be furious, but we're getting very good at picking up clues. I'll think of something.'

At breakfast Jilly and Steve stoked up on black coffee and Anadin. Julius said, 'Are we going to let her take the albums this time?'

'From what you've discovered,' Steve said, 'none of them is hers to take. But if her heart's set on it, I suppose we'd better.'

'And the loose photographs?'

'Yes. You can put them back in the albums first and she'll never know they were missing.'

'I think she's already seen them,' Jack said. 'It was years ago, but she'll remember them.'

'You have a theory about this too?' Jilly said, staring at the two of them. 'Have you worked out what happened?'

'We think so,' Julius said. 'We may know so by this afternoon. Come on, Jack, let's put the photographs back, and the postcards.'

'She's not getting the postcards, is she?'

'No, and she's not getting the oldest albums either, the Stopford–Gethin ones. They are nothing to do with her, they're pre-Cowgill.'

'It's a pity she's getting the others,' Jack said. 'Those are *our* history too.'

'Yes, well,' Julius said, 'some of those albums have pockets on the inside back covers. That's where they kept the negatives – including the UFO one. I've taken them all out.'

'And what about the fiver?'

'I think she ought to have the whole package,' Julius said. 'I think she ought to *see* it, at any rate, just so she'll know that someone was sorry. I'm going to wrap the photos in it again.'

Then he took *The Straight Way from Oxenford* and laid it on the table with the photograph albums.

'Is that for a sort of trap, to take her by surprise?'

'Not really,' Julius said, 'but if we show her Tom's first book we can casually and naturally ask her about the second one. I'll make sure we're in here when she comes looking for the albums.'

*

After Julius's contrite speech, Jack was almost ready to feel sorry for Auntie Bat. The feeling dispersed when she opened the door, walked into the library and stopped short at the sight of them sitting at the table.

'What are you doing in here?' she said.

'We've been listing the books for the inventory,' Julius said truthfully, for that was exactly what they had been doing. 'Look, we found this. Is it by Uncle Tom?'

Auntie Bat crossed the room and snatched the book from his hand all in one movement. 'Where did you find this?'

'On the shelf,' Jack said, pointing, but he was watching Auntie Bat and noticed that she had relaxed as she opened the book and read the title. Clearly, she had expected it to be a different book.

'What happened to the other one?' he said boldly.

'Which other one? There is no other one.'

'There's a review clipped out of a newspaper in there,' Julius said, 'between pages 34 and 35. It says he was preparing another book.'

'No one will ever see that book,' Auntie Bat said. 'It does not exist. Robert did the only decent thing, under the circumstances, not that that did any good. But not a copy survived. I watched the fire myself. Now, where are the albums?'

Julius nodded at the pile.

'I understood there were more.'

'Not that you would want. Just our family.' Julius silently handed her the packet of photographs, wrapped up in a five-pound note. 'And we found these too.'

Smiling bitterly, Auntie Bat took the packet from

him and opened it. Then she folded it up again and slipped it into one of the albums. Jack waited for her to say something but she did not, so instead he said, 'They *were* sorry, you know. John was. Afterwards.'

'John was a guest in our house,' Auntie Bat said. 'When the letter came from Dorothy he was there. I never understood how Dorothy could have been a party to it. Everyone was sorry, too late. Far too late.'

She turned and went out.

'She doesn't know what we know,' Jack said.

'Yes, she does, but she doesn't know we know it. And I don't really think she even knows who we are. We're just The Enemy,' Julius said sadly. 'The sins of the fathers shall be visited upon the children. And the sins of the grandmothers and great-uncles.'

When Auntie Bat had left in a hired car, not in a removal van, Jilly came into the library.

'Poor old thing,' she said, looking round, 'she's as loopy as Tom was, by all accounts.'

'Tom was loopy? You never told us.'

'You didn't ask. Well, think about the alien-visitors story. It doesn't sound exactly sane, does it? He had a nervous breakdown and killed himself, just before Steve was born.'

Julius smacked his forehead with the flat of his hand. 'It was the flying saucer,' he said. 'Jack's father knew about that. And you know he committed suicide. Why didn't you tell each other?'

'We've hardly had the chance,' Jilly said.

'Well, now we know the whole story,' Julius said. 'We'll tell you this evening.'

'Can't we wait till Mum and Dad get here?' Jack

said. 'Dad wants to know too. More than anyone.'

'Let's fit it together this evening,' Jilly said, 'all four of us, and see if we can fill in all the gaps, and then tell Peter when he arrives on Sunday.'

The fire was lit again in the living room and after an early supper they gathered round it. In a dark corner two metres of Leyland cypress loomed out of a bucket of sand and twinkled with fairy lights.

'I'll tell it,' Julius said, 'and Jack will correct me if I go wrong, and if you two have any bright ideas you can tell us, OK?

'OK. When Nellie Ackroyd was a little girl she was given a state-of-the-art camera, a Box Brownie, and she photographed everything in sight. In August 1910 she went out for the day with her big brother Alfred, and some of his friends, Cecil and Josephine Cowgill and Maud Aylward. They went to Clifton Hampden and Goring and a place somewhere in that area called Edgebury Castle or Colman's Camp on Edgebury Hill.

'While Nellie was taking a photo at Edgebury Castle the wind blew her hat off and she got a snap of the other four running after it and pointing. When she put the picture in her album she wrote under it, *Alfred, Cecil, Maud, Josephine and unidentified flying object, Edgebury Castle, August 1910.* Just as you said, Jilly, it was a joke, right?'

'Right.'

'Later on Maud married Cecil Cowgill and they had two children, Thomas and Patricia. Alfred died in the First World War and Cecil in 1925. We don't know where Josephine went but she was dead by 1947. Maud

168

died in 1938. Nellie grew up and married Maud's brother Robert and became our great-grandmother. She inherited this house and they lived here with their four children, Richard, Dorothy, Jeremy and John. And by this time everyone was taking snapshots and sticking them in the albums, and some of them were terrible. The point is, Tom and Pat never saw the albums. Tom had never seen the albums when he got interested in the theories of Alfred Watkins and wrote a book about ley lines.

'After the war – the Second World War – Dorothy goes to America for a visit and gets engaged, we think, and while she's there – and this is where the facts stop and the guesses begin – while Dorothy is in the States she hears about two things: Kenneth Arnold, the man who first described alien spacecraft as saucers on 24 June 1947, and the Roswell Incident eight days later, where people reported a disc-shaped object crashing in the New Mexico desert. There was talk of alien beings in the wreckage.

'When Dorothy comes home for the last time, there's Tom with his ley-line investigations around Edgebury Castle and – this is where it gets really theoretical,' Julius warned them, 'we think that Tom did see a UFO. Or thought he did. And maybe the others thought Tom was a bit of a nerd, or they just didn't like him, but anyway, Dorothy wrote to Richard, who was in Berlin, and told him what was going on. Richard remembered the Edgebury Castle photo and some other odd things in the albums, and got his youngest brother, John, to take them out and send them to him, and then he sent them to Tom. Tom and Pat were up in Harrogate by this time. Richard sent John five pounds for his trouble, or the postage, I don't know; but anyway, Tom fell for it, the proof of the photographs, and put them in his second book. And I think he wrote to his Aunt Nellie and said, "Did you really see a UFO at Edgebury Castle in 1910?" By this time Alfred, Cecil, Maud and Josephine were dead. Nellie was the only one left. And she told Tom, yes, she really had. Joking. I don't know if she knew what was going on or not. It's not the kind of thing grandmothers do,' Julius said severely, 'but, of course, she wasn't a grandmother yet.

'Anyway, the book got published and Dorothy, back in the States, heard about it and wrote to Tom explaining that he'd been hoaxed. Maybe she felt guilty. I hope she did. John was there in Harrogate, with the Cowgills, when the letter came. He didn't know what had been going on, how he had been used; when he found out he sent the original photos, and the fiver, back to Richard. He was so angry he wrote, "I never want to speak to you again, you swine."

'When Robert found out what they'd done – we're guessing here, but Auntie Bat said as much – he bought up the whole print run and burned it, so there was no trace of Tom's book, or the hoax. But it was too late. Tom never got over the way they'd made such a fool of him and had a breakdown and killed himself, and Auntie Pat's never forgiven anyone who was involved. And they never forgave each other.'

'Give or take a detail,' Steve said, 'I should imagine that you are absolutely right. Congratulations, both of you.'

'What a miserable story,' Jilly said.

'We don't know what was in the second book, of course,' Julius said, 'but we guess it was something to do with flying saucers homing in on ley lines. And landing somewhere near here. And aliens getting out and hanging around being photographed.'

'I'd give anything to know what he wrote,' Steve said.

'The awful thing is,' Julius said, 'if he'd only waited a few years, everyone else would have been saying it too. There was a sort of flying-saucer shower over France in 1954 and in the 1960s someone else came up with the theory that ley lines and flying saucers were connected. Tom was just, well, born too soon.'

'Yes,' Jilly said, 'even if it was all eyewash, at least he would have been in good company.'

'It's not what he wrote I want to read,' Julius said, 'I want to know what he saw. There must have been something to start him off, and this time it wasn't a hat.'

'We'll never know now,' Steve said. 'Auntie Pat will take the secret to her grave. And Robert bought up every copy and burned them, did he? I call that heroic.'

'Robert was the good guy,' Julius said. 'I think that's why Auntie Pat came to his funeral.'

'I'm not surprised that none of them ever spoke to each other again,' Jilly said. 'A joke that got out of hand. I wonder what he did see.'

Jack said, 'GG might not have burned *every* copy.'

'We'd have a hell of a job tracking one down if he didn't,' Steve said. 'We don't even know the title. If we advertised for the works of Cowgill we'd be inundated with copies of *The Straight Way from Oxenford* and never a sniff of the one we want.'

'Not advertise,' Jack said. 'In the Bodleian. Julius says they've got a copy of every book ever printed in Britain.' He looked at Steve. 'And he said you could get in there.'

Chapter Twelve

'**I** don't believe this!' Julius shouted. '*Shut?*'

'Till next week. It's a library, remember. Librarians need holidays too. I'll get in as soon as they open again, I promise. In the meantime, why don't we go out and see if we can find Edgebury Castle?'

They fetched the maps and laid them out to compare notes.

'The newest one has a metric scale,' Julius said, flourishing the ruler. 'The 1919 one is the same as 1830 – one inch to the mile – but a straight line is a straight line, so if we just keep going through East Hagbourne and Blewbury, here we are . . . where it says *Fort.*'

'It's almost on the Ridgeway,' Steve said. 'Barely a stone's throw from here.'

'It isn't marked as the Ridgeway on the oldest map,' Jack said, 'but it does show Edgebury Hill. Look, here. And in 1919 they thought it was a Roman camp.'

'They thought Aston Upthorpe was a Danish camp,' Julius said. 'Personally, I don't think they had a clue about what any of them were. They might just as well have been Hollow Hills full of fairies. Anyway, Tom used the old name for his earthwork, Colman's Camp. Well, he would, wouldn't he? Colman the surveyor, who lit the beacons.'

'It's so close,' Steve said. 'All we have to do is drive to Streatley and follow the Ridgeway. The whole area's a network of footpaths and bridleways.'

'And contour lines,' Jilly said. 'This is going to be an up-and-down affair and I smell snow in the wind. Wrap up warm.'

Even the oldest map, with its ominous black shading instead of contours, had not prepared them for the ups and downs that lay ahead of them. As they drove through Watlington and Benson and headed south for Streatley, Jack watched the horizon, expecting Edgebury Castle to loom up as the Sinodun Hills did, but the downs on the Berkshire side of the river rolled luxuriously from valley to valley, and the road followed the lower slopes so closely that there was no way of guessing what lay concealed above them.

'I think we need the next turn to the right,' Julius said. 'It looks like a road – no, not that, it's a farm track.'

When they found the turning, that too was scarcely more than a track. It had been a metalled road once but now the steep surface was broken and pitted into an assault course for vehicles.

'We'll never get up that,' Jilly said, sounding suspiciously hopeful.

'There's tyre tracks,' Julius said. 'Somebody gets up here. Can't we just try?'

Steve took the car up very slowly, limping from rut to pothole, with thorny branches scraping their flanks on either side.

'Don't forget we have to come down again,' Jilly said, looking gloomily through the rear window, but suddenly the track widened into a grassy plateau surrounded by trees and tall bushes.

'Out,' Steve said. 'Everybody out. We'll walk from here. We're either on the Fair Mile or the Ridgeway itself. Lowbury and Edgebury lie between them.'

The path was wide and level now; the hedges and woodland began to thin out. Through the gaps familiar landmarks came into view: Wittenham Clumps and Didcot Power Station. They were walking on the summit of a chalk down and the land sloped away on either side, more hills to the left, the Thames Valley to the right.

'There's a footpath along here,' Julius said, running ahead and calling back. 'It doesn't say where it goes but there's something up there on the other side of the valley – that sort of enclosure with the hedge round it.'

It took another twenty minutes to cross the valley, but at last the path took them to a gap in a hedge with a stile across it. On the far side of the stile a sheer turf bank reared up, pocked with rabbit holes.

'I think this is it,' Julius said, vaulting the stile, and they scrambled over behind him, to find themselves on a rough rectangle of grass surrounded by sky, except at one end where there stood a low terraced mound.

'We're here,' Jack said.

It was so small. Jack walked the perimeter in a couple of minutes before he joined the others on the mound. First he paused at the foot and looked all around, seeing what Nellie Ackroyd had seen as she stood there with her Box Brownie camera, eighty-five years ago, and wondering what Tom Cowgill had seen in 1948. He would not have seen Didcot Power Station, fuming away in the distance, the pylons, the white grazes in the sky where aircraft began their descent into Heathrow. But he had seen something, something that had started him off on the strange, sad theory that led to the terrible trick played on him by his cousins, and to his own death, by his own hand.

'Coming up?' Julius said.

Jack turned and climbed.

'Iron Age or Bronze Age, I'd guess,' Steve was saying. 'A very minor local chieftain with his own earthwork and look-out. The big business went on over at the Sinodun Camp.'

They could see again the Sinodun Hills, the clumps of trees on the double crest. What they could not see was a clear line to Didcot through Blewbury and East Hagbourne. A shoulder of the downs obscured the view.

'There must have been another ley mark on that next ridge,' Julius said, 'and they would probably have had to light beacons to fix it. Alfred Watkins thought "ley" came from the old word for light. Beacons were lit to light the way. Colman was the man who lit the beacons. Perhaps this is what they did here.'

'I think we'll never know,' Steve said. 'Everyone has

his own pet theories. Some people believed that when the British Isles were first invaded the original inhabitants, who were small and dark – the Cymru – were associated with these mounds, which of course they were, and that's where the idea of a race of little people, fairies, came from. Alfred Watkins thought of straight tracks; that's a perfectly sensible idea, even if it's wrong. There's no reason why Iron Age Man or even Stone Age Man wouldn't have wanted to travel in straight lines. There's nothing particularly eccentric about taking a short cut. Forget the beams of cosmic power and flying saucers.'

'That's just the latest theory,' Julius said, 'that and crop circles. Poor old Tom, just got going too soon.'

'Poor old Tom,' Jilly said. 'Who knows, if we stick around long enough it may turn out he was right. We'll come back here when your family arrives, Jack. They'll want to see the scene of the crime.'

New Year's Eve was thick with fog. When Mum, Dad and Marty finally arrived, it was late and Jack had been half expecting the police to turn up with news of a fatal accident, but at last, looking out of the window at the end of the landing, they saw lights approaching from further up the hill, where the fog was thinner, and then swerving in at the gate in twin eerie haloes.

'Alien touch-down,' Julius said. 'You know, if weather conditions were right, Tom may have seen something perfectly normal and it just looked uncanny. But you'd think, wouldn't you, that if aliens did survive the journey from Alpha Centauri and navigate to exactly this little blot on the universe, they'd have the technology to land where they'd meet sensible people, like Heathrow for instance. If a flying saucer turned up there, they'd clear a runway for it fast enough. Customs and Immigration would be over like a shot.'

They went down and found Marty already in the hall, already talking; Mum and Dad following with overnight bags and gift-wrapped bottles.

'Into the living room quick,' Jilly said. 'Huge fire, food laid out, eat first and then Jack and Julius will tell you the whole story. It's not a very happy story, I'm afraid,' she said to Dad, as she took his coat, 'but if it's any consolation, everyone was very sorry afterwards.'

'You're serious?' Dad said. 'They really have found out what happened?'

'Oh, yes,' Jilly said. 'I'm afraid they have.'

It was the following week when the letter came from Julius. It was in a thick manila envelope, and arrived just as Jack was leaving for school. He stood looking at it, undecided.

'Wait till this evening,' Marty advised. 'Don't rush through it now and spoil your day because you can't pay attention to anything.'

'It's not just a letter.'

'It's not a book either,' Marty said, squeezing it, 'so Steve hasn't been robbing the Bodleian. Leave it. Go on, you'll be late. Don't even open it.'

He could not concentrate at school anyway, knowing that perhaps the last part of the puzzle was waiting for him at home. Usually when he came in he had a drink and then went to his room to get his homework out of the way. But homework could wait tonight.

He was the first one in. He made himself coffee and went upstairs to where the envelope lay, as he had left it, on his desk. The address was written in Julius's dashing capitals. He slit the flap carefully and drew out the contents.

They were several sheets of paper, stapled together, with a note from Julius.

The book is in the Bodleian and Steve has had some of it copied. All but three of the photos were in it. Ring me when you've read it.

He settled down. The first sheet was the title-page. *We are Not Alone* it was called, by Thomas Cowgill, author of *The Straight Way from Oxenford*. The next sheet read:

My thanks are due to the Aylward family of Stoke Crowell Manor, Oxon, without whose help the writing of this book would not have been possible. I must particularly thank Richard Aylward for supplying invaluable photographic evidence, and Mrs Elinor Aylward for sharing her memories of a remarkable incident.

It was worse than they had thought. Not only had the Aylwards hoaxed Tom, he had publicly thanked them for doing it. Jack turned to the next page and at last found out what Tom Cowgill had seen all those years ago at Edgebury Castle.

INTRODUCTION
In the following pages I hope to expound my theories concerning various remarkable sightings at the ancient earthwork of Colman's Camp on Edgebury Hill, Berkshire. Since 1936 I have been

conducting searches for ley lines, or prehistoric straight tracks, in the Thames Valley, and while being fully aware of how few 'real' archaeologists would agree with my findings or those of other members of the Straight Track Postal Portfolio Club, I have never discovered anything that would cause incredulity among informed and sensible opinion. I say 'never', but on 2 February 1948 I witnessed a phenomenon which has convinced me that we, in the mid-twentieth century, are on the cusp between the prehistoric and what I can only describe as the protohistoric, that which lies before us.

It has been vouchsafed to many for more than half a century to observe the entry into our atmosphere of aerial craft from unknown sources, perhaps from other worlds lying within and without our solar system. In the last year the United States of America has been 'host' to at least two visits from such unidentified craft. On 24 June 1947 Kenneth Arnold of Washington State saw from his private aeroplane strange craft which he described, when asked, as resembling saucers being skimmed across water. A week later this was followed by an 'incident' at Roswell, whence came reports of a 'disc' or 'saucer' which had crashed near to this New Mexico town.

Like so many who have 'heard but not seen', I was prepared to discountenance these reports until I encountered a phenomenon which no amount of scepticism will dispel. In modern Christian Britain 2 February is Candlemas, its very name implying the nature of the Celtic Fire Festival it has supplanted, Imbolc. On my newly discovered ley at Colman's Camp, Berkshire, I wished to observe the alignment with the rising sun and bicycled over to the mound at dawn and there waited, well wrapped in rugs with a Thermos of hot, sweet tea against the bitter cold of this upland site.

He *was* a nerd, Jack thought sadly, and imagined Tom Cowgill, serious in his spectacles and bicycle clips, wrapped in a blanket and sitting on Edgebury Castle, waiting for the sun to rise.

The sunrise itself was obscured by trees and I sat waiting for the fiery orb to appear above the spinney. I cannot believe that in such cold I could have fallen asleep, but I was aware of a trance-like sensation, a numbness followed by a tingling.

Energizing white fuzziness? Jack wondered.

Alert at once to the legends of misfortunes that befall those who linger on 'Hollow Hills', especially on 'festal days', I prepared to stand up, and at that moment beheld the phenomenon. Directly ahead of me in the sky, which was clear except for milky cirrus clouds, I saw abreast three brilliant lights approaching at low altitude. As I watched they blazed more fiercely and merged together in one vast glowing sphere. Cursing myself for not having my camera 'at the ready', I fumbled for it in my knapsack. When I looked up again the – what can I call it but a phenomenon? – had vanished in the thickening cloud. Seeing a cyclist approaching in the lane at a little distance, I raced down the mound and along the footpath, hailing him as I went.

'Did you see that?' I cried, as we met.

'See what?' the cyclist replied.

'The lights in the sky over there.'

'Well,' said this Berkshire worthy, 'most mornings the sun do come up over there, but I sees no lights at all today.'

Tom trying to be funny was worse than Tom being serious.

Since there was no one at home, my sister having removed from our house in East Hagbourne to Harrogate, I cycled at high speed to the home of my cousins over the border in Oxfordshire. My aunt and my cousin Dorothy were surprised to see me so early in the day, but welcomed me in and listened while I told my amazing story. As I was speaking I noticed them looking at me strangely and then Dorothy said, 'Why, Mother, that would not be the first time that mysterious things have been seen over Colman's Camp.'

That was the end of the page. There was no more. But it was enough to be going on with. Jack could just imagine the scene. Peculiar Cousin Tom raving about his phenomenal lights in the sky, while Dorothy and her mother, Nellie, raised their eyebrows at each other, both thinking of the same thing: the photograph that Nellie took in 1910.

He went down to the telephone and dialled the Stoke Crowell number. Jilly answered.

'Jack? Julius isn't home yet. He has to get back from Wallingford. I take it the letter's arrived.'

'Yes, it has. Have you got any more of the book?'

'A bit, but Steve can't very well get them to Xerox the whole of it at once. It may be the only copy left in the entire world, but it's still in copyright, believe it or not. What do you think?'

'I don't know. I mean, he saw something, didn't he? Flying lights . . . and it was daylight. If he'd seen it after dark it might have been an aircraft.'

'Steve and Julius have a theory about that – hang on. I think that's Julius coming in now.'

There were muffled calls at the other end of the

line, a clatter and then Julius picked up the phone.

'You've got the copies?'

'Yes. Jilly was just telling me you have a theory.'

'It's Steve's, really, but he doesn't know the half of it. I've been doing some research today. Steve thinks that what Tom saw was a parhelion.'

'You what?'

'It's a phenomenon, all right, a meteorological one. The conditions were right, Tom describes them. It was very cold, thin cirrus cloud, right?'

'Yes.'

'When that happens you often get optical illusions, sun glories, sun dogs and that. The ice particles in the clouds refract the light and you get the appearance of a second sun, next to the real one. Very rarely, you get a *pair* of sun dogs, one each side: a triple sun.'

'Do you think Steve's right? Tom *was* looking towards the sunrise, wasn't he?'

'Yes, but he didn't see it because the trees were in the way. And he was half asleep, or he had a nip of something he hasn't told us about in his tea, even if he did think he was experiencing cosmic forces. He probably nodded off, and when he woke up, there was the blazing vision in front of him.'

'The awful thing is,' Jack said, 'he never thought of flying saucers till he went and told Nellie and Dorothy. They must have been the ones who started all that. *He* just thought he was seeing mystical Celtic fires. What was your research?'

'Nothing cosmic,' Julius said, 'but a very odd coincidence. Cast your mind back to 1461.'

'I wasn't actually around in 1461.'

'Nor was I. Anyway, it was during the Wars of the Roses, a clash between the armies of Edward Plantagenet and Margaret of Anjou, at a place called Mortimer's Cross in Herefordshire. Early in the morning the Yorkists, that was Edward's lot, saw three suns in the sky that merged and became one.'

'What Tom saw.'

'Exactly what Tom saw. The army didn't know about light refraction – nobody did in the fifteenth century – and they thought it was a terrible omen, but Edward said no, it wasn't, it was a wonderful omen and it meant they were going to win. And they did. And afterwards, when he became King Edward IV, he took the parhelion as part of his personal badge. It was called the Sun in Splendour.'

'Didn't Tom know about that?'

'Why should he? You didn't, nor did I till Steve told me about the parhelion. Then I put two and two together and remembered the Wars of the Roses. Still, that's not the coincidence. It's a very rare phenomenon, but other people have seen it. No, the coincidence is, it was on the same day.'

'The same day as what?'

'The second of February. That was the day Tom saw his flying saucer and it was the day when Edward Plantagenet saw the Sun in Splendour. And Tom was right about Candlemas too. It used to be Imbolc.'

'What is Imbolc?'

'The ancient Britons, or Celts or Cymru or whoever, had four fire festivals: Beltane, that was May Day Eve; Samhain, which has got shared out between Hallowe'en and Guy Fawkes Night – bonfires, you see;

Lughnasa, which became Lammas, Loaf-mass, a sort of Harvest Festival; and Imbolc, which was the end of the winter solstice, 2 February, and New Year's Day for the early Christians. Remember, the calendar was different then. It's also Groundhog Day, but we won't worry about that.'

'If only Tom had known,' Jack said, 'if only he hadn't spoken to Dorothy and Nellie. He'd have been quite happy looking for fire signs on Imbolc, or seeing the Sun in Splendour. It would have made his day.'

'He wasn't interested in history or weather,' Julius said, 'only prehistory and phenomena. But Steve says that he was a cryptanalyst during the war, decoding the Enigma ciphers at Bletchley Park. They worked under terrible pressure and Steve reckons that Richard let everyone think it was that that caused his breakdown. Only, of course, a lot of people knew it wasn't that at all – and there goes the blood feud again. But he went straight from Cambridge to Bletchley, and apparently he really was a bit odd after the war.'

'So when Dorothy heard him wittering on about lights in the sky, she remembered hearing of Kenneth Arnold, the first time she was in the States, and led him on.'

'It seems a lot of Allied pilots reported seeing UFOs flying alongside them during the war. They called them foo-fighters.'

'Is *that* what a foo-fighter is?'

'You know what,' Julius said, 'we could do a book about this – no, seriously, desk-top publishing, *A True Account of the Events at Colman's Camp in 1948*, and lay poor Tom's ghost to rest. I've kind of got to like him, even if he was an anorak. We can work on it at half-term. When is your half-term?'

'Give us a chance, we only went back to school on Monday,' Jack said. 'Hang on, there's a list stuck to the fridge. We pack up on 17 February.'

'So do we,' Julius said. 'Right, it's a date. Have you got a bike?'

'Yes.'

'Bring it with you. We'll go ley-hunting,' Julius said. 'We'll go up to Colman's Camp and try to fix Tom's ley from start to finish. It's in the book, Steve says, and there *is* a sixth marker. And who's to know what we may see? After all,' he added, 'there's just a chance we've got it all wrong, isn't there? Perhaps Tom really did have a close encounter. Had you thought of that?'